THE SPANISH PAPERS

THE SPANISH PAPERS

A DAN KOTLER ARCHAEOLOGICAL THRILLER

KEVIN TUMLINSON

PRINT EDITION ISBN: 9781386909613

ALSO BY KEVIN TUMLINSON

Dan Kotler

The Coelho Medallion

The Atlantis Riddle

The Devil's Interval

The Girl in the Mayan Tomb

The Antarctic Forgery

The Stepping Maze

The God Extinction

The Spanish Papers

Dan Kotler Short Fiction

The Brass Hall - A Dan Kotler Story

The Jani Sigil - FREE short story from
KevinTumlinson.com/joinme

Citadel

Citadel: First Colony

Citadel: Paths in Darkness

Citadel: Children of Light

Citadel: The Value of War

Colony Girl: A Citadel Universe Story

Zero

Collections

Citadel: Omnibus

Uncanny Divide — With Nick Thacker & Will Flora

Light Years — The Complete Science Fiction Library

YA & Middle Grade

Secret of the Diamond Sword — An Alex Kotler Mystery

Wordslinger (Non-Fiction)

30-Day Author: Develop a Daily Writing Habit and Write Your
Book In 30 Days (Or Less)

Watch for more at kevintumlinson.com/books

PROLOGUE

Mesa, Arizona

Motes of dust drifted and swirled in a slant of sunlight allowed grudging passage through the filthy window of the old shed. It was the primary light source for the shed, during the day. A lamp picked up the slack when things got dark.

The shed itself was hardly worthy of the name. It was a patched and rickety pile of wood and nails, more of a lean-to against the cinder wall at the back of the property than a structure standing all on its own. In fact, the shed was built mostly of rotting plywood and two-by-fours, anchored to the cinderblock wall that may have been the only thing keeping it standing.

It would be considered hazardous by the standards of the city, and badly in need of a good fire by the standards of Ricky's kin.

His grandfather had built the shed more than seven decades earlier and hadn't put much stock in fancy modern conventions, such as building codes or architectural best practices. He knew how to make a pile of sticks stand up for 70 years, though, so that was something.

Anyway, it was Ricky Miller's inheritance, and the only one he'd ever gotten. And he put it to good use nearly daily.

Somewhere along in its history, someone had decided to install electricity in the shed. Though *install* was maybe too strong of a word for it, Ricky figured. The shed's electrical grid, in its entirety, consisted of a weathered, orange extension cord that had been stapled in place along the rafters, terminating at two grounded sockets in a molded orange rubber nub, affixed to the wall just above the workbench. The cord had been cut, spliced, patched and taped so many times over the years, it resembled a sort of rag-doll garden snake, slithering in through a grime-filled gap in the cinder block wall and trailing along the plywood ceiling like it was preparing to drop down and strangle its prey.

It wasn't pretty, and it was likely a fire hazard, but it at least gave Ricky the means to plug in the table lamp he'd rescued from the curb. It only added a weak amount of light to the space, but at least he could move it closer.

Ricky was holding the lamp like a torch, letting the naked incandescent bulb cast light on something he couldn't quite wrap his head around.

Spread out on the wooden workbench, among a scattering of hand tools and fishing lures, were three sheets of old, tan-colored paper. The sheets had handwriting on them, and though they were tough to read, Ricky figured the writing was Spanish.

Each page had its straight edges, but also a torn edge along one side like they might have been ripped out of a book at some point.

Ricky didn't know much Spanish, but he could recognize a word or two. He couldn't really make heads or tails of what little he could read, though.

But there were a few things on these pages that needed no translation.

There were drawings—sketches. And he recognized some of it.

Ricky was a local history buff. And local history, in Mesa, *A-Z*, meant the Hohokam—a long-gone tribe of Native Americans who had lived in the Sonoran Desert before the Europeans showed up and started causing troubles for the natives. Here locally, the Hohokam were run off or killed off, it was hard to know for sure.

The ruins and leave-behinds of the Hohokam had earned them their name back in the '30s. An archaeologist named Harold S. Gladwin had chosen the name for its irony. *Hohokam* was an O'odham word that meant "all used up" or "those who are gone." It wasn't clear which meaning Mr. Gladwin had in mind, but the name had stuck.

Gone people, was how Ricky thought of them. He'd thought that was clever because it sounded like the titles of all those books they sold at the Dollar Save. He'd picked up a couple of them on grocery and beer runs but hadn't read any of them yet. He preferred history.

Ricky wasn't an archaeologist by any stretch, but he had studied the Hohokam as a personal hobby ever since his retirement, and he knew Hohokam artifacts and symbols when he saw them. And right now he was seeing plenty.

Most of the sketches were Hohokam objects, including bits of what looked like handmade jewelry and carved stone statues, bowls, and other utensils. There was a lot that Ricky recognized, and a lot more that he didn't.

But the thing that had Ricky's undivided attention was something that didn't look Hohokam at all. In fact, it looked like something that shouldn't be anywhere near the Sonoran Desert, particularly in Mesa, Arizona.

It was a drawing of a rocket ship.

The thing was cigar-shaped, with wings on either side and a finned tail that ended in a fanned cone. To Ricky, it looked like a rocket booster. He'd seen things like this when he was in the Army. Though not *exactly* like this.

It was just about the most 50s-looking rocket design Ricky could imagine. Like the toys he had when he was a kid, and the TV shows from that time. *Flash Gordon* and *Buck Rogers*. This thing looked a little like a shuttle, but it didn't have the stubby nose or the landing gear.

It was completely out of place—a rocket ship from a time when nobody would even know what a rocket ship was. And what really set it apart, Ricky figured, was that it was covered in symbols and drawings just like the designs on the Hohokam jewelry and pottery. A Hohokam *rocket*. He could hardly believe it. In all the years that he'd studied up on the Hohokam, he'd never once seen anything like this. Not here. But he'd seen something like it somewhere else.

Ricky had watched plenty of *Ancient Aliens*. It was practically the only show the History Channel ran these days, and it interested him. It made him curious about all the weird coincidences in ancient cultures—the links between the Egyptians and the Mayans and the Aztecs. All of them supposedly had nothing to do with each other, thousands of years ago. But then there were the pyramids and snake gods and legends about this or that, and it was all very similar. There were symbols carved into temples in Egypt and Central America that looked like tanks and helicopters and rocket ships.

It was all too much to ignore, Ricky thought.

Aliens were real, as far as he was concerned, and he figured the government knew all about them. The government knew a lot it wasn't telling people. Aliens and lizard people and secret mind control technology—Ricky had heard it all and believed most of it.

These papers might prove something like that, Ricky figured. Maybe prove that aliens existed, and they built the pyramids and Stonehenge and all of it. Maybe the History Channel would pay him something for them. Maybe they'd let him meet that dude with the hair that looked like a riled turkey. Maybe, Ricky thought, he'd get on TV.

That was a lot of maybes in one place, and if his grandpa had taught him anything, it was never trust a maybe. Trust what your eyes could see and what your ears could hear, and what your hands could hold. Right now, Ricky was holding something that might or might not have anything to do with aliens, but by his estimate, was a significant archeological find. Something that might make him rich and famous.

Ricky was retired. He was living on a pension and what little savings he'd managed. He was eating bacon and cornbread for most meals and washing it down with tap water. He could use some extra money coming in, and it wouldn't be too shabby to have his name on the news and in the history books, either.

Wouldn't that get the attention of his family? Bunch of no-goods never respected him and never would. Unless he got famous. They'd come around asking favors then, he knew. And he could tell them all where to go.

He carefully put the lamp down and gathered the pages. They had been preserved in a leather pouch, which was weathered but had fared pretty well, considering. The storage unit he'd found them in hadn't been climate controlled, but the dry air of the desert had helped keep things from rotting or falling apart.

Just to be safe, though, Ricky put the pages back in the

pouch and then put the pouch in an ice chest along with a container of marine desiccant. That would keep the humidity down, just in case. For double good measure, he sealed the ice chest with duct tape. And to keep any looky-loos out of it, he used a Sharpie to write "mule deer stool samples, do not turn over." He had no reason to keep such a thing around, but snoopers might not know that.

He turned then to his laptop—a barely-working Dell that his boy had given him and set up for him. Ricky opened his email and typed in the address he'd found online.

There was a man—an archeologist, according to his LinkedIn profile. Dr. Dan Kotler. He wasn't a professor and wasn't with any universities or museums.

But he spoke at a lot of places. He'd even done one of those TED Talks. And he was known to answer emails from strangers, and to look into new things found by amateurs who might not know what they had.

Ricky had seen him in an interview on the History Channel, maybe even on *Ancient Aliens,* though he wasn't too sure about it. But Dr. Kotler was talking about ancient cultures and artifacts, and how they were all connected somehow. And it was him that found that Viking city in Pueblo, and that island that might be Atlantis. So Dr. Kotler was legit. He seemed nice, but he also seemed open to almost any idea.

Ricky typed out his message with two fingers and then attached photos of the pages before he hit send.

A day later, he got a reply.

Dr. Kotler responded and asked a few questions. Just sort of following up, getting things clear. There was a lot there, and Ricky was starting to wonder if he'd made a mistake, showing these pages to somebody he didn't really know. But the email ended with three sentences that made Ricky smile:

I think you've found something significant. Send me your address. I'm boarding a plane for Mesa in an hour.

1

DR. DAN KOTLER was used to getting cryptic and strange messages via email. He had a special email address just for the purpose, and it was publicized just about everywhere. He used a service to cull through the crackpots and the attention seekers, to help him cull down the pile. Occasionally there was a death threat or some sort of stalker-like missive, and his team took care of it, reporting it to the authorities. They were pretty good at clearing away the rubble and forwarding on the messages that mattered.

This one mattered.

It wasn't the email itself that had piqued Kotler's interest, but the photos. Six images of three torn pages, front and back. The handwriting was in Spanish, which he was able to read with little trouble. And there were drawings, hand-sketched explorations of Hohokam symbology and artifacts. These were fascinating all on their own—a relatively detailed study of a handful of pieces from a lost culture. The mail service knew he'd be interested, and they were right.

And there was that rocket ship ...

That was the phrase Ricky Miller had used, and Kotler was inclined to see his point. The sketch certainly looked like a spaceship, complete with a booster and tail fins. The fact that it was covered in Hohokam symbols made it all the more intriguing.

Kotler had seen similar objects before, even among Hohokam artifacts and dig sites. The "rocket" resembled the Quimbaya airplanes—Colombian artifacts that dated as early as 1,000 BC and gaining some notoriety in 1994 after a team of aeronautical engineers built a model airplane based on the design. The model was able to fly—demonstrating an understanding of aerodynamics from a civilization that disappeared a thousand years before the Wright Brothers were born.

To Kotler, however, the design more closely resembled common artifacts among the Hohokam. Archaeologists had recovered hundreds of pieces of jewelry, crafted mostly from shale, carved into the shapes of birds and insects. This design was a bit more elaborate and had more Hohokam symbology worked into it. Kotler couldn't rule out an *Ancient Aliens*-like theory of prehistoric space travel, but he wasn't quite prepared to accept it as fact just yet.

What compelled Kotler to book a flight and get to Mesa as quickly as possible came less from potential alien influence and more from the description, handwritten in Spanish, in a paragraph next to the sketch.

Alongside descriptions of some of the Hohokam objects they were sketching, the author of these journal pages had also written the phrase *División Azul*—the Blue Division.

That caught Kotler's attention because it helped to date these pages. And the date wasn't quite as ancient as Ricky Miller had hoped. It was, however, even more intriguing for its implications.

During World War II, while under dictatorial rule by General Francisco Franco Bahamonde, Spain did all but ally itself with Nazi-controlled Germany. As a way to repay Germany for its aid during the Spanish Civil War, Franco offered to allow Spanish citizens to volunteer for service on the front. The caveat was that Spanish troops would only confront Communist Russia and no other Western Allies.

It was a fine line, and it was apparent that Franco was playing both sides. He wanted to please Hitler, to absolve the debt between their countries. He wanted to push back the advance of the Russians, who had been a threat for decades. But he also wanted to keep his options open with the Allies, just in case. Spain had to keep up its trade and relations with the West, after all, regardless of who won in this conflict. It was impossible for Spain to remain entirely neutral, but they could limit their exposure.

Hitler agreed to Franco's terms, and Franco commissioned a new military branch—the Blue Division—to rise in defense of Spain against Russian intrusion. On behalf of Nazi-controlled Germany, of course.

Consisting of some 18,000 men, and including its own Air Force squadron, the *División Azul* became Hitler's best weapon against the Red Army. The Blue Division was so proficient, in fact, that Hitler commissioned a unique medal to award to its members, for efficiency in routing the enemy on the Eastern front.

It seemed Franco's half-hearted commitment was paying off. And Blue Division continued operation until 1943, when it was finally ordered to withdraw and disband, largely at the request of the Roman Catholic Church.

When Kotler spotted the reference to *División Azul*, in connection to North American native artifacts, he immediately wanted to know more. And since he had some time on his hands, he figured this was as good an opportunity as any to take a little vacation of sorts.

Kotler and FBI agent Roland Denzel had returned home from an excursion in Egypt nearly a month earlier, a bit battered and bruised, and somewhat unsure of what would happen next. Their adventure in Egypt had been unique in several ways, not the least of which was the presence and exploration of an elaborate Druidic archeological site in the mountains of Egypt, and the discovery of a vast, underground ecosystem referred to as the Otherworld.

During those events, both Kotler and Denzel were abducted by members of a cult calling itself *Alihat Iadida*— The New Gods. Kotler had encountered them once before, years ago and under a slightly different name, though he hadn't realized just how powerful the organization had become.

Powerful enough that it had been able to recruit both members of the archaeological team on site, and a Captain of the Egyptian military, along with his men, all providing security on location. The implications were frightening. The reach of the Alihat Iadida was far more significant than Kotler would have expected.

Once they were back stateside, both Kotler and Denzel endured an elaborate debriefing that included both the FBI and the State Department. Compared to some other debriefings Kotler had been subjected to, this one went very smoothly. Denzel had officially been on vacation, and Kotler had been invited by the Egyptian government to oversee operations at the site. Neither had known of the actions of the Alihat Iadida, before arriving onsite. Both had been abducted and forced to comply against their will with the demands of the rogue military unit. It was all pretty straightforward, considering.

What had not been revealed was Agent Denzel's willingness to hand over one of the site's artifacts, in ransom for Kotler's life. Thankfully anyone who was aware of that exchange was either dead, imprisoned, or on their side. But even if it had been revealed, Kotler was pretty sure they could mitigate it. The move had been strategic, as part of an effort to save Kotler's life. And a result of the plan, an entirely new level of historical exploration had been uncovered.

At the moment, Dr. Kotler was very popular with the Egyptian government, having uncovered this plot and discovered a new archaeological gold mine, in the process.

His popularity, of course, had not extended to allowing him to stay in Egypt to oversee exploration of the new site. But by the time he'd arrived home, he was more than ok with that outcome.

He'd come to some conclusions, while in Egypt.

The first was that, though he enjoyed participating in dig sites and explorations, he was no longer content with the notion of overseeing such a site full-time or long-term. Kotler was associated with several archaeological sites worldwide, some of which he'd helped to discover. Many of these were tied to his consulting work with the FBI, which gave him a particular perspective that he'd lack otherwise.

That led to the second conclusion. Though he'd had some setbacks over the past two years, with threats to his life becoming alarmingly regular and mundane, he'd also grown fond of his work with the FBI and had discovered something of a personal mission.

He had, in just over two years, helped the FBI to take down multiple terrorists, to recover a trove of lost historical artifacts, to dismantle a powerful smuggling operation, and to thwart the plans of would-be conquerors and emerging world powers. Not bad for an anthropologist with no academic affiliation.

The events in Egypt had given him something to consider. His work with Historic Crimes—the FBI division headed by Agent Denzel—gave him access to a world that few others would ever see. It allowed him to not only explore the mysteries of ancient world cultures but to make a difference on the modern world stage. Through his work at Historic Crimes, Kotler could put his talents and abilities to good use, for the benefit of humanity. It was a lofty idea, which just added to its appeal.

Kotler had also determined that this work with the FBI was furthering one of his long-standing personal ambitions.

Kotler had spent his life in pursuit of answers to certain questions. Science and history had been his primary tools of exploration, in all that time. He had a background in anthropology, but also in quantum physics and a few other fields. He was a practiced and astute observer of humanity, from its ancient practices to its modern-day psychological nuances. His background in science gave him insight into the mechanics of the universe as well. And all of it had been cultivated toward one purpose: Kotler wanted to understand.

He was seeking the *meaning* for humanity, and humanity's role in the greater universe. He had studied everything he could find in this pursuit and had embraced history and cultural studies as the primary key to his goals. But he'd come to realize that applying what he was learning to the here and now, assisting Agent Denzel and the FBI to help preserve humanity against those who would seek to dominate or destroy—that was gratifying on a level he'd never expected. And it was giving him new insight into the answers he sought. He was learning, as he helped to solve these cases.

And so he'd decided that he would stay as a consultant to the FBI. He would continue to be a part of Historic Crimes, and he would use it as a tool for finding more answers while helping to protect humanity itself.

Noble and altruistic ideas, he knew. And maybe they were all part of some sort of self-aggrandizement. Kotler certainly had ego to spare. But he was also sincere in his pursuit, and in his empathy for others. For now, this was a good fit for his life and his career and his ambitions. He believed he could find answers here.

As his flight was approaching Mesa, Arizona, he contemplated another aspect of his decision.

He was not going to limit himself merely to the cases the FBI brought to him. There were more questions out there that he was uniquely capable of solving. Not all of them were the result of terrorists or smugglers or secret cults. Some were just the sort of challenges that only someone like Kotler could resolve.

Of course, it didn't hurt to have a little help from a US federal agency.

He had been using his iPad to do a bit of research on the Hohokam and the Blue Division when a text message popped up from Agent Denzel, back in Manhattan.

You left in a hurry, Denzel wrote.

Kotler smiled and responded. *I've had my fill of government offices for the moment. Got something interesting from my email service. I'm headed to Mesa, Arizona.*

Will you be gone long? Denzel replied.

Not sure, Kotler wrote. *I'll be in touch. Anything going on?*

I have something I thought you might be interested in, but it'll keep.

Kotler considered for a moment before responding. *Send me details. I'm meeting with someone in Mesa to look over some papers he's found. I don't think it should take too much time. I can look into whatever you have when I get a chance.*

Kotler watched the screen as the pulsing set of dots appeared, indicating that Denzel was typing a response. It must have been a doozy, as things were still pulsing when the Captain came over the intercom to tell them they were about to land.

The in-flight WiFi must have been shut off in preparation for landing, and Kotler tucked his iPad into his bag and returned his tray to its full and upright position, just as the flight attendant asked. He'd check in on Denzel's message once he was on the ground.

The landing went smoothly, and Kotler moved through the airport quickly. He had arranged for a rental car while in the air, and at the rental counter, he went through the requisite requirements of filling out paperwork, handing over credit cards, and going on the hunt for his rental.

He forgot about Denzel's message, in the shuffle, and focused on finding his way to Ricky Miller's home.

2

"Found 'em when I was picking through a storage unit I bought at auction," Ricky said as Kotler peered over the papers.

They were sitting in Ricky's kitchen, at a worn and chipped Formica table that seemed as if it might once have been in a diner. A lot of Ricky's possessions seemed to be repurposed rescues, from the vintage post office box attached to the frame of his front door to the Coca-Cola beverage cooler being used as a refrigerator. Ricky seemed to be from that cut of humanity's cloth that wasted nothing and salvaged everything.

Lucky thing, too, Kotler thought as he scanned over the papers as well as the leather pouch that had contained them.

"Do you know anything about the previous owner?" Kotler asked, looking up.

Ricky shook his head. "Not really. A lawyer, I think. Died a few months ago, and no one came to claim his lot. I paid fifty bucks for it. No one else wanted it. Full of old clothes and animal heads."

"Animal heads?" Kotler asked, confused.

"Trophies," Ricky shrugged. "Guy was a hunter."

Kotler nodded. "Did you find anything else in there?"

Ricky shook his head. "Nothing useful, and nothing like this," he motioned to the pages. "I went back through all of it after I found that. I thought the leather pouch was empty at first. It was dark in there, and when I opened it, I didn't notice those. I was going to use it as a tool pouch or something, out in the shed. Or maybe cut it up to use the leather. But then I saw those and the rocket ship, and I knew it had to be about the aliens."

Kotler fought the urge to laugh or even smirk. He didn't want to offend Ricky, who appeared to be a true believer. It was just that it caught him off guard to hear aliens get so casual a mention.

It wasn't that Kotler didn't believe in aliens—the universe was a strange place, and they'd only explored it to the width of a hair, in relative terms. They had peered into the void through the equivalent of a keyhole and had only seen vague shadows on a cave wall. It gave humanity a sense of what was out there, but no actual answers. Not yet.

But Kotler found he really appreciated Ricky's take on this.

It was just that Ricky had already made up his mind about what this was, and what it represented. An armchair archaeologist who wanted to believe. He did his own work, and his own research, without anyone's help and without any need for the approval of others. In the end, he and Kotler weren't so different.

"I'm going to be honest with you .... I'm not so sure this is aliens. But that doesn't make it any less fascinating."

Ricky was nodding. "What about that rocket ship?"

Kotler also nodded. "That's pretty interesting. And I'm

THE SPANISH PAPERS 19

not saying it's not a rocket. There are artifacts resembling this in a few Mesoamerican cultures. We're still working out what they mean. But what brought me out here was something written here next to the sketches." Kotler pointed to a section of handwriting. "División Azul. It translates to 'the Blue Division.' Are you familiar with that?"

Ricky thought for a moment. "Spain," he said. "They worked with the Nazis."

Kotler smiled and nodded. "Exactly. So you can see why this is a fascinating find. Why is there a mention of a World War II Spanish squadron scrawled next to a sketch of a Hohokam artifact? That's the kind of riddle I like." He grinned, and Ricky joined him.

"So even if it ain't aliens, it's something big," Ricky said.

Kotler could see in the man's body language that he was excited by the prospects of this. Mostly, Kotler figured, he was interested in some sort of payday. And Kotler thought he might be able to arrange that, even if it meant paying the man a little something out of his own pocket. If this led to a paper or some other publication, Kotler would happily give Ricky Miller all the credit of discovery, if he wanted it.

"Ricky, can I take these with me? I want to take them to someone for authentication and analysis. I can leave you with a voucher, as proof that you had these and that I'm borrowing them."

"Well ..." Ricky said, angling his head. "You see, Doc, vouchers don't really pay for much, now do they?"

Kotler did laugh then and shook his head. "No, they don't. So you're looking to sell them?"

"I did pay for 'em," Ricky said. "They're my property."

Kotler nodded. "Alright. I don't normally buy artifacts—it's kind of an ethics thing. But how about this: I will pay you a commission for reaching out to me with this. If you'll allow me to take these for authentication, and if you agree to let me pass them along to a museum or institution for study and display, I'll promise to make sure you are listed as the owner and donor. They'll remain your property, and I'll help make arrangements for compensation and insurance, whatever comes of them."

Ricky blinked. "That's ... I appreciate that,"; he said. "I wasn't expecting anything like that. I figured you'd just pay me off and take credit for finding 'em."

Kotler smiled and shook his head. "I don't operate like that. So how much did you have in mind?"

Ricky turned his face away slightly, as if suddenly ashamed of what he'd planned to ask for. He gave a slight shake of his head.

"Go ahead," Kotler said. "You're not going to offend me. Tell me what you think is a fair rate, and I'll pay it as a commission."

Ricky looked at him, considering. "I was going to ask for twenty grand," he said.

Kotler considered this for a moment, then reluctantly shook his head. "I can't pay you twenty grand for this," he said.

Ricky looked a little deflated but nodded, as if he'd over-reached.

"It's worth far more than that. I'll give you fifty grand. That's your commission, and if this goes on display some-where, I'll arrange for you to be compensated as the patron. Sound fair?"

Ricky looked at him like he was a talking tree stump but nodded. "More than fair, I'd say." He was excited, Kotler could see, but holding it together. Then, pausing and considering, he asked, "Why would you do this?"

Kotler had his reasons. Mostly, as he looked around at

THE SPANISH PAPERS 21

Ricky's place, he felt the retiree could use the money. But it went beyond that. He'd only known Ricky for an hour or so, but he liked him. He could sense the man's loneliness and even a bit of his anger. He had described his home as his inheritance, and he'd talked about his living relatives as if they wanted nothing to do with him. Kotler could relate.

Kotler's brother, Jeffrey, had recently cut off nearly all communication, after being caught up in one of Kotler's cases. Jeffrey had been abducted and chained to a wall, with a bomb strapped to his chest, by one of Kotler's former physics professors. It was all part of an elaborate plot to steal government secrets and to exploit a cache of historical documents from the early days of the NSA. It was understandable that the experience had left a bad taste in Jeffrey's mouth. Kotler wasn't sure if the rift between him and his brother could ever quite be bridged, but he remained hopeful.

So sympathy and empathy, more than anything, were making Kotler act.

"I want you to get what's fair," Kotler said. "I don't always have a way to make things fair. But this time I do."

Ricky watched Kotler's face during this exchange and nodded. Whether he understood the nuances of what Kotler was feeling, there was no way to tell. But both men were fine with letting an unnamed and unacknowledged connection pass between them.

Kotler gathered up the pages, gave Ricky a check for the full amount, and then asked for any and all information he had on the storage unit. Ricky gave him some names and addresses, mostly for the auction house and the storage building's owners. It was a start.

Kotler bid Ricky farewell, promising to keep him updated. As he climbed into the rental car, he closed the door and rolled down the window. "Ricky ... don't tell your family about the money."

Ricky laughed. "You kiddin'? I ain't tellin' anybody about the money. My bank's only going to know about it 'cuz I can't deposit it otherwise."

Kotler smiled. "Take care, Ricky. I'll be in touch."

With that, he pulled out of Ricky's driveway and started toward town. Within the hour he was checked into his hotel room. He'd only brought a backpack with a few essentials, including a change of clothes. He preferred traveling light when he could.

He was taking his toiletries out, intending to shower and rest up so he could start following some leads on the papers in the morning.

His phone buzzed.

With a start, he remembered that he hadn't checked Denzel's message, once he'd gotten to the ground. Everything had moved pretty quickly since landing, and between meeting Ricky and studying the papers, Kotler had never actually looked at his phone.

He picked it up now, noting that there were two messages from Denzel and one from Liz Ludlum.

Liz was saying she hoped he had a good trip, and that she missed him. He smiled at that. The two of them had only just started dating and weren't yet past the get-to-know-you stage. They were still shy and sweet with each other, which was nice. Kotler knew that he was keeping the pace of their relationship slow, for a lot of reasons. But he missed her too. He sent her a note to say so. He promised dinner and a night on the town when he was back.

He glanced through Denzel's message.

Got some leads on the Alihat Iadida. Made a definite connection to the other group you told me about, in Scotland.

They're the same bunch. And we found links to some local branches, here in the US. We're still looking into it. I'll let you know what we find.

Then, the message that had just arrived:

Not sure if you got my last message, so I sent via email. But something else has come up. I got a call from someone there in Mesa. Local authorities. They wanted to know why the FBI was sending a consultant without alerting them ahead of time. What exactly are you telling people?

Kotler was confused. He tapped in a reply.

I haven't told anyone anything, he wrote. *Haven't even talked to anyone, aside from the rental car people and the man I flew in to see. Did they say how they knew I was here?*

A moment later. *They said you came in flashing your FBI credentials, demanding anything they had on some guy named Ricky Miller.*

Kotler felt his heart pound. *Ricky Miller is the man I came to see. But I never talked to the authorities here. I didn't even bring my FBI credentials. Forgot them in my rush to pack. This wasn't me. But now I'm worried about Ricky.*

Denzel responded, *I'm booking a flight. I can be there in a few hours. Stay put.*

What about Ricky? Kotler replied.

I'll ask the locals to go check on him.

Kotler considered for a moment. *I'm going out there,* he wrote. *Tell them I'll be there.*

Kotler just stay put, Denzel wrote.

Tell them I'm there, he replied, and slipped the phone in his pocket as he made for the door.

He paused, his hand hovering over the door handle, and then turned back to his bag. He fished out the leather envelope and the pages, then opened the closet. There was a safe inside, and he took the papers out of the leather envelope and put them inside before locking the safe door with a code. He then dug back through his bag and found some pages of notes. He shoved these into the leather envelope and then left it on the small desk.

It was a precaution. He wasn't even sure if it would be necessary. But someone was here in Mesa, impersonating him and looking for Ricky Miller. It wasn't a stretch to think they'd come here. The Spanish papers were the only connection Kotler could think of. If someone was after them, then it seemed in everyone's best interest to keep them hidden. He hoped they'd be secure enough in the safe.

In a rush now, Kotler left the room, making sure the door was secure behind him. He rode the elevator to the ground floor and paid the valet to let him tag along to where his car was parked so he could leave in a hurry.

He prayed that Ricky was safe.

In his gut, he felt as though his prayers might be in vain.

3

Liz Ludlum had just gotten back from a run when her phone buzzed. She saw Kotler's message and smiled. It was nice. It was also safe. She shook her head.

She and Dan Kotler had flirted for a good long while before that first kiss, after an adrenaline-fueled encounter with a Russian assassin. Since then they had dated, in a casual, almost chaste sort of way. Which wasn't so bad, considering. She knew Kotler had a reputation for being something of a womanizer, and she had no intention of being someone's conquest.

Though Kotler's proclivities had changed a couple of years ago. His name was still in the papers, but his photos had far fewer women in evening gowns draped on his arm. These days he was getting more attention for his academics than for his presence on the social scene.

And more, Kotler had poured himself into his work over the past two years in a way that bordered on obsessive. Some of that might have been due to the increased notoriety and credibility that had come as a result of being associated with a handful of significant discoveries. Some may have been the result of his work with the FBI, and the challenges that presented. But Ludlum could see that something had changed in Kotler over the past two years, mainly when it came to his relationships.

Ludlum couldn't be sure if it was Evelyn Horelica or Gail McCarthy who had put Kotler into a romantic tailspin. He and Evelyn had already more or less split before things really went sour, during the events in Colorado. Evelyn had been a rock for Kotler—a relationship he'd come to depend upon to the point of taking it for granted.

When Evelyn had cut things off, after her abduction and rescue, it had disrupted Kotler somehow. It had awoken something in him, Ludlum thought. It made him realize that he was vulnerable, and that games of the heart made everyone a loser, in the end.

Evelyn Horelica's leaving had made Kotler realize what he was missing out on.

But Gail McCarthy ... she had done more than break Kotler's heart.

For the better part of two years, Gail McCarthy had played mind games with Kotler, while also toying with the FBI and every other US alphabet agency, plus dozens of law enforcement agencies worldwide. Gail had been the heir to a vast smuggling operation—potentially the biggest in history. She was brilliant, driven, and from what Ludlum could determine, a complete sociopath.

Before any of that had come to light, however, she and Kotler had been involved. And though it turned out to be the first of many head trips, Kotler hadn't quite gotten past it.

It was made worse, doubtless, by the fact that it was Kotler who had been forced to kill Gail, to protect Agent Denzel and to prevent her and her smuggling operation from becoming an even more significant threat to the world. Kotler acted as if he'd gotten past this, but Ludlum thought he was just in denial, not dealing with it.

Ludlum was giving him time. And space. She wanted him to deal with the things that might prevent their relationship from being everything it could be.

But her patience was wearing a little thin.

This trip to Arizona, for example, was just another example of the challenges of being Kotler's girlfriend. Not only was he prone to picking up and traveling with no notice, his travels invariably led to trouble. She hoped this time would be different. And she hoped that he'd come around to thinking about her, communicating with her, before packing a bag and sending her a quick text on his way to the airport.

Time, she decided. She could give him time. For now.

Ludlum showered and dressed. It actually worked out that Kotler was out of town. It was evening, and she'd left the FBI offices for the day, but there was still work to be done. She still had her side project.

Tonight she was meeting with Dani—Agent Danielle Brown—to dig deeper into origins of Historic Crimes.

A month ago Ludlum had met with a man in Central Park. He'd kept things mysterious and clandestine—like a scene from a Tom Clancy novel. Ludlum had gone in with Agent Brown as backup, but it was entirely off the books. Which meant it was both dangerous and, possibly, quite stupid. But it had yielded fresh leads at a time when any leads were in short supply, and that made it worth the risk.

Historic Crimes—the FBI's new division for investigating history-based cases that might present modern-day national threats. The department was run by Agent Roland Denzel, who had first met Dan Kotler during the incident in

Pueblo. The two of them had helped thwart a terrorist plot to detonate a dirty bomb under NORAD, and it had all been tied to a medallion that linked several Native American tribes to a newly discovered Viking presence.

For their first adventure together, it had undoubtedly set the stage. Denzel had recruited Kotler as a consultant to the FBI, and together they had solved hundreds of cases, big and small, and brought down some truly frightening threats.

The question that Ludlum and Agent Brown were asking, however, was pretty straightforward: Why "Historic Crimes?" And connected to that, why Dr. Dan Kotler?

Ludlum and Dani had taken it on themselves to answer these questions, to see if they could determine who was behind the charter for the department, and why it was so crucial that Historic Crimes exist. They were looking into the department's funding, into its apparent autonomy, its origins, and its history. When the man in Central Park had approached them, it became clear that they were asking questions that someone might not want answered. And so they'd decided to take the investigation off book.

Ludlum checked herself in the hall mirror. She was dressed in black—casual but worthy enough of a club if that had been her destination. She could blend into a Manhattan nightlife crowd, at any rate, and that might prove useful.

She glanced down to the table under the mirror and saw her grandfather's medical bag.

It was her most valued possession. And she knew it made her something of an anachronism among her peers, as she visited crime scenes. When she was a Lead Forensics Specialist for the NYPD, she'd gotten a reputation because of that bag—it had gotten her noticed. And under that notice, her superiors realized she was very good at her job.

The promotions came, and new opportunities came with them. Standing out a little worked well for your career, she'd decided, if you could also be outstanding in your work.

Now in her role with the FBI's Historic Crimes division, there weren't as many wide eyes or curious expressions. The FBI could be a little more formal than the NYPD, with fewer cliques and boys' clubs. Standing out tended to be more about excellence than accessories. But the bag still marked her as somehow eccentric, and that helped her make inroads for the respect of her peers.

These days, she thought of the bag as a reminder of her heritage. Her grandfather would be proud of her and the career she'd built, she knew. That was the real reason she carried it—to honor him.

Of course, in a division that included Dan Kotler and a flood of ancient artifacts, secret passages, and mysterious codes, her eccentricity was just a drop in the ocean anyway. Everyone working Historic Crimes had become inoculated to eccentricity and just focused on doing their jobs.

Ludlum wouldn't need the bag this evening. She was doing a different sort of forensic work on nights like this. Work that required her to talk to dangerous people about even more dangerous things, and to open doors that someone didn't want opened. For this work, it was best to blend in as much as possible. Standing out might get her and Agent Brown killed.

She left her apartment, using the app on her phone to activate the series of locks she'd recently installed. Along with these, she turned a key in a couple of more traditional locks as well. None of this was impenetrable by any stretch, but it all made her feel better. She'd taken to being a bit paranoid lately, as a best practice.

Down on the street she waited for an Uber and took this

to a spot about three blocks from her actual destination. From there she started walking, ducking into a couple of local cafes and bars, taking back doors into alleys before continuing on. More paranoid precautions, but she and Dani had agreed that this was necessary. In fact, Agent Brown herself was doing something similar, coming in from the opposite direction.

Ludlum arrived at the storage facility and used her code to let herself in. She and Dani had chosen this place for its security, including the grid of cameras that tenants could access via an app. Ludlum checked the cameras, seeing herself enter through the access door. No one else appeared to be in the building.

Ludlum made her way to the unit they were renting, opened the lock and slipped inside, pulling the door down behind her. Once inside she slid a bar into place, which prevented anyone else from lifting the door. She would be able to check the cameras when Dani arrived, and let her in.

Elaborate. Clandestine. Even a little stressful. But all of it was necessary. Ludlum and Dani were taking every possible precaution to throw off anyone who might be tracking them, after the cryptic warning they'd received from the man in the park.

Of course, the warning wasn't the only thing they'd gotten from him.

The storage unit was set up like a small office, with a couple of tables serving as desks and folding chairs where they could sit. Power was supplied from the socket of an overhead light, with lines running down the unit's walls and to power strips on the table tops. Plugged into these were bits of equipment—mostly defunct and decommissioned gear that Ludlum and Dani had bought used, paying cash. But one piece of equipment was brand new.

In the center of everything was a laptop, its lid folded closed and only its power cable attached. They'd bought this from a random local retailer and had made some specific requests for modifications. It had no wireless card, and thus no way to connect to a hotspot, intentionally or otherwise. In fact, there was nothing in the machine that would allow it to connect to the internet or any other network at all. It was completely isolated.

They were running an open source Linux operating system, stripped of anything that could track keystrokes or try to access the internet, though this was just an extra layer of protection.

The computer was "air-gapped," meaning it was physically incapable of going online or otherwise being accessed remotely. It had never been connected to a network, wirelessly or otherwise. It was, in effect, the only safe way to look at data without worrying about hackers or spies. One would need literal, physical access to the machine to get to its data. And even then, there was no data to find.

For extra security, nothing was stored on the laptop itself. Instead, everything they were using was stored on an encrypted thumb drive, given to them by the man in the park. There were no copies. Ludlum had the only drive.

Ludlum reached into her blouse and removed a small, gold pendant. She pulled the bottom and top sections apart to reveal the tiny thumb drive and pinched the drive between her thumb and forefinger to remove it.

She kept it on her at all times, so that she was always aware of where it was. Even when passing through security at FBI headquarters, she kept it always in sight as she moved through the scanners. The guards knew her and knew she was with the Bureau, which helped. But the pendant was just about as innocuous as any piece of jewelry could be. No one gave it a second look.

Now she put the thumb drive into the air-gapped laptop and opened the files she'd been scrutinizing for weeks.

Her phone buzzed, and she glanced down. Dani was entering the building. In a moment there was a light rap on the storage unit's door, and Ludlum removed the bolt and opened it enough for Dani to duck under and enter. She closed and bolted the door again.

"Sorry I'm a little late," Dani said. "Agent Denzel had to leave for Arizona at the last minute."

"Arizona?" Ludlum asked. "Does it have something to do with Dan? He's in Arizona right now."

"Doesn't it always have something to do with Dan?" Agent Brown asked.

Ludlum smiled and shook her head. She worried about Kotler. A lot. But she also knew that there were few people more capable than him when it came to dealing with trouble. She also knew that Agent Denzel would always have Kotler's back. Whatever might have the two of them off gallivanting again, she was sure she'd hear all about it soon.

For now, she and Dani pulled up chairs and got to work.

Dani had her leather attaché with her and opened it to pull out a series of files. She put these on the desk, and as Ludlum started turning through them, Dani said, "These were tougher to come by than the last batch. Some of them are the closest matches I could find to the stuff on the thumb drive. It would have helped a lot if our mystery man had given us more than just case file numbers for this kind of thing."

"There's a lot that would make this easier," Ludlum said. She opened one of the folders and referenced its file number to the information onscreen. "Ok, this one," she said. She read the extract from the front of the file and shook her head. "This is a pretty minor case. Stolen evidence. Some of it pretty old. It might have been an early Historic Crimes case if the department had been around then."

"What's the year?" Dani asked.

"1985. The case went cold. No leads, no suspects."

Dani considered this. "A cold case from 1985. What about the others?"

Ludlum scanned through the remaining files, and all were similar. "All cold cases. All thefts involving historical artifacts. What good does this do us?"

She leaned back, leaving the folders open on the table and staring at the information on the laptop.

Dani started going over the case files, standing up to give herself more mobility and spreading them out to look at them side-by-side. She shook her head after a moment. "That's the only connection I can see. The types of crimes. The artifacts themselves are all over the place. Maps, documents, objects from different points in history and different regions. I think most of these were only on the FBI's radar because of their monetary value."

Ludlum leaned forward, looking closer at the laptop's screen. "The case numbers are from different lots and eras, too. There doesn't seem to be anything connecting these ..." she stopped mid-sentence.

"Found something?" Dani asked.

Liz looked around and found a notepad and pen. She placed these on the table in front of the laptop and began scribbling, referencing the screen from time to time.

She held up the list she'd made. "These are the names associated with the cases. Basically the victims of these thefts. Or the organizations that reported them, at least. Notice anything?"

Dani looked at them, and at first, shook her head. Then it clicked. "None of them are individuals. All of them are ... what? Museums maybe?"

"This one," Ludlum said, pointing. "Baker Tait. That's an auction house. I know that one because I helped in the investigation of a murder there. A woman ... I can't remember her name. But I know the lead detective on that case. Detective Holden."

"Holden?" Dani said, making a face. "I think I know that case. I heard about it, anyway. But Holden ... he was also involved in that thing with Ashton Mink. The whole 'Devil's Interval' thing."

"And Baker Tait was the auction house that procured those items from Edison's estate," Ludlum said. "The first case Gail McCarthy was involved in. The first case that was officially on the docket for Historic Crimes. Where all this started."

Dani leaned in, looking over Ludlum's notes. "What artifact was stolen, in association with Baker Tait?"

"Several," Ludlum said, running her fingers down the list. "In fact, all the names on this list get repeated pretty often. There's definitely something going on there."

Dani thought this over. "Ok. I think we might want to visit at least one of these." She shook her head. "But if I go in any official capacity, it could lead to some backlash. We need a way in that won't raise suspicion."

Ludlum thought this over, then smiled. "I think I have a way," she said.

4

IT WAS dark when Kotler arrived at the scene and parked his rental car to the side of the gravel road. There were three cars in the drive, two police cruisers and a sedan, blocking access. Kotler exited and approached slowly. He really wished he'd remembered to bring his FBI credentials, but at the moment they might not benefit him.

He introduced himself to the two uniformed officers. "I was here earlier, visiting Ricky Miller. Is ... is he ok?"

The officers exchanged glances. "What did you say your name was again?"

"Kotler," he said. "Dr. Dan Kotler. I'm a consultant with the FBI."

"Got any ID?" one officer asked.

Kotler showed his ID, and the officer took it and went inside. Moments later a man wearing a brown suit and a loose tie came out, holding Kotler's ID and staring at it as he walked. The man stood in front of him and handed the ID over. "Dr. Kotler?"

Kotler nodded. "I left here a few hours ago. I got a call from an associate, Agent Roland Denzel of the FBI. He said there'd been someone claiming to be me, at your local offices."

"There was," the man said. He showed his badge. "I'm Detective Brian Kozak, Mesa PD. I ... spoke with you when you came by our offices." He grinned at this as if it were quite the joke. But Kotler caught a glimpse of something in the Detective's eyes. A hard edge that told Kotler he might be in some trouble here.

Kotler nodded. "Obviously that wasn't me. But he had my FBI credentials?"

"He did," Kozak nodded. "And he was pretty convincing. So you'll understand if I don't exactly take your word for things, ID or no ID."

Kotler shook his head. "What do I need to do? I can put you in touch with Agent Denzel. He's actually on his way here, on the first flight he could get."

Kozak considered this. "I think maybe it'd be best, then, if you stayed with me until he gets here." The detective paused for a moment, his expression hardening. Kotler could read in his face that he was distrustful, maybe even a little angry. Maybe over being fooled? "Or I could have you escorted to a cell."

"A cell? Detective, last I checked I'd have to at least be a suspect in a crime to justify something like that. If someone else used my identity, that doesn't make me a criminal."

"No," Kozak said. "But if you were the last person to see Ricky Miller alive, you may be a suspect in his murder."

Kotler blinked and felt his heart thump. "Murder?" he whispered. "Ricky's dead?"

"Looks like it happened a few hours ago. We got an anonymous tip. Someone called it in and said they'd seen you leaving here in a tear."

"A tear?" Kotler laughed and shook his head. "No. I was

here at Ricky's request. I can show you our emails. I came here to ..." he hesitated. "Discuss something with him."

"And what would that be?" Kozak asked.

Kotler shook his head. "I think it would be best if I had someone present when I discuss this."

"A lawyer?" Kozak asked, his expression changing to something smug and knowing, as if he'd been expecting Kotler to lawyer up.

He thinks he has his man, Kotler realized. *He figures me for this.*

"I was thinking Agent Denzel," Kotler replied.

Kozak nodded and indicated to the two officers that they should take Kotler into custody.

Kotler went willingly, allowing himself to be cuffed and placed in the back of one of the cruisers. He sat for a long while, his hands behind him in an uncomfortable position.

A few hours later the police emerged, from Ricky's house and Kotler was driven to Mesa, where he was placed in a room to wait some more.

It was going to be a long night, and Kotler was beginning to wish he'd stayed in his hotel room. The police would have arrived eventually, but by then he'd have been fed, might even have gotten in some research on the Spanish papers.

The moment he'd heard that someone was looking for Ricky Miller, however, he'd gotten a bad feeling. Learning that Ricky was dead was heartbreaking.

Kotler resolved that regardless of his discomfort and his growing impatience with the Mesa PD, he was going to do everything he could to find Ricky's killer.

Assuming he wasn't thrown in jail while this whole thing was sorted out.

· · ·

WHEN DENZEL FINALLY ARRIVED, he didn't seem pleased. He sat next to Kotler and asked the officer on duty to remove Kotler's cuffs.

The officer hesitated, and Denzel scowled. "I'm an FBI agent, which your boss spent more than an hour verifying. This is my partner. I'm armed. You're armed. He's harmless. Open those damned cuffs and stop trying to screw around with me."

The officer opened the cuffs and then left Kotler and Denzel to chat.

"Detective Kozak is an asshole," Denzel sneered.

"I hadn't noticed," Kotler said, rubbing his wrists.

"He'll be in here in a minute. How are you doing?"

Kotler shook his head. "I'm a little shaken. Ricky was a good guy. He didn't deserve what happened to him."

Denzel huffed and was about to say something when the door opened and Detective Kozak entered. He dropped a folder on the table, attempting to startle them both, it seemed. Kotler casually reached out without waiting to be told and opened the folder.

"That's Ricky Miller with three bullet holes in him," Kozak said. "Close range and personal. So I need to know where you were when they got there."

"My hotel room," Kotler said. "I left Ricky's place and drove straight there. It wasn't more than an hour before Agent Denzel contacted me to say someone had been impersonating me here, and I went straight back to Ricky's place. That's when I met you and life became sublime."

"Cute," Kozak said. "So you're saying that at the time Ricky Miller was being shot, you were actually driving to the hotel?"

"I'd say that's probably about right," Kotler said.

"Which hotel?" Kozak asked.

Kotler gave him the information. "They can verify my check-in time."

"Fancy place," Kozak said. Kotler noted the hint of a sneer, suppressed but not by much.

Kozak looked at his notes and shook his head. "The timetable on this stinks. What time did you say you left Ricky's place?"

"Maybe 6 p.m. I'm pretty sure I checked into the hotel a little after seven."

"We got our call at 5 p.m.," Kozak said. "A 911 call that I have on tape, telling us that Ricky Miller was dead and that you'd just left the scene."

"Kotler left the scene?" Denzel asked. "They specifically said Kotler?"

Kozak made a show of rechecking his notes. "Dr. Dan Kotler," he said in a sort of sing-song tone.

"And how, exactly, did they know it was Kotler?" Denzel asked.

Kozak shrugged. "Guy's kind of famous, isn't he? On TV? Folks around here watch a lot of TV, especially those History Channel shows. Not much else to do out where Ricky lives. Lived." He pointedly at Kotler. "So your timetable isn't smelling too good, Dr. Kotler. You want to change any details?"

"Why would I want to change details?" Kotler asked. "Let's talk about motive. I had none. Why would I kill the man I'd just flown all this way to see?"

"Maybe he showed you something you didn't want him to have," Kozak said. "You shared your emails. Thank you for that. We're looking those over now."

Kotler nodded. "So you know what I came here to see. Those papers."

"And where are those papers now?" Kozak asked.

"In my hotel room. In the safe," Kotler responded.

"I'm going to want to see those," Kozak said. "I'll have some of my people go retrieve them if you don't mind."

"You're going to need a warrant and me in the room," Kotler said.

"And me," Denzel added.

"Oh, I'll have the warrant, you can relax about that," Kozak said.

He turned back to the folder on the table and flipped through the crime scene photos, pulling one out and tossing it in front of Kotler and Denzel. "Did you buy those papers off of Mr. Miller?" Kozak asked.

Kotler looked and saw that the photo was of the check he'd written, made out to Ricky Miller. "Not exactly," Kotler replied. "I wasn't buying them from him. I felt that would be unethical. I was paying him a commission for contacting me about them, and as a way to compensate him. He was letting me take them for verification and analysis, and I wanted him to feel more comfortable about it."

Kozak listened but was nodding the whole time Kotler spoke. "Fifty-thousand dollars. That's a lot of money for some old papers, isn't it? You always give people money like that?"

Kotler shook his head. "No, that's not a typical thing. Honestly, I thought Ricky could use the money, and I felt for him. A retiree, living on scraps. It ... well, he reminded me of someone I know. Aside from that, this find has some significance."

"I'd say so," Kozak said, smiling. "Fifty-thousand—that's a lot of significance, for sure. Seems like that would be a good way to cover your tracks if you were a rich guy who'd just killed a man to get what he wants."

"Now wait a damn minute," Denzel started, leaning forward with his hands on the table.

Kozak ignored him. "That hotel you're in, that's pretty pricey, too, isn't it? You make that kind of money, consulting for the FBI?"

"I have my own means," Kotler replied.

He didn't have to be skilled in reading body language to see that Kozak was making a play. He had Kotler figured for this, for sure, and he was building his case.

"Your own means," Kozak repeated, nodding.

"There's nothing illegal about anything Dr. Kotler did in this case," Denzel said. "You know that as well as I do. So what's your play here, Detective? What's the real reason you think Kotler was involved in this?"

Kozak shrugged. "Maybe I just don't like how any of it smells, Agent Denzel. I get one guy claiming to be Dr. Kotler, waiving an FBI name tag in my face and demanding I give him everything I have on Ricky Miller. And then a few hours later Ricky Miller's dead, and another Dr. Kotler was the last person to see him alive. A witness puts him there at the time of the death. That's enough for just about anybody to get suspicious, don't you think?"

"An anonymous caller," Kotler said.

"Sorry?" Kozak asked.

"It was an anonymous caller, not a witness," Kotler said. "Do you have anyone willing to go on record to say they saw me there? That Ricky wasn't alive when I left?"

Kozak smirked and shook his head. "No, Dr. Kotler, I don't. You got me there. But my team is asking around right now. It's pretty wide open and empty out there, so people think they can get away with a lot, like no one's watching. But everyone out there sees everything, all the time. So it's not going to be long before we can corroborate this."

Kotler thought about this. "Detective, I think you've decided to make this personal."

"Personal, huh?" Kozak said, his jaw working. He smirked and shook his head. "Yeah, Dr. Kotler, I'd say I take it real personal when some New York asshole comes to town and murders one of my citizens."

"Oh, I'm sure I'm an affront to everything you think about yourself," Kotler said. "But I think you're more angry over the fact that you got duped."

Kozak said nothing but watched him, his eyes hard and angry.

"Someone came here pretending to be me, and you gave them information that led to the murder of Ricky Miller. You're feeling like a sucker, and you've decided that it doesn't matter who goes down for this, as long as it's me."

Kozak said nothing for a moment, then laughed and shook his head. "I'll do my job, Dr. Kotler. I'll follow the evidence, and I'll find my man. I just happen to think my man is you, at the moment."

Kotler considered this and nodded. "OK, charge me."

Kozak said nothing but glared at him, the half-smile still on his lips.

"Or release him," Denzel added.

Kozak glanced at Denzel and shook his head. He spoke to Kotler. "Don't leave town. In fact, I'd say don't leave your hotel."

"I won't leave town," Kotler said. "I'll promise that much. I'm going to stay right here until I know who murdered Ricky."

"Yeah," Kozak said, the smirk back on his lips as he stared Kotler down. "Me too."

5

POLICE WERE ALREADY in Kotler's room when he and Denzel arrived at the hotel. The officer in charge handed him the warrant as they approached and barred him from entering the room.

"Would you give us the combination to the safe?" The officer asked.

"No," Kotler said. "But I will open the safe."

The officer glared but stepped aside and allowed Kotler into the room.

The place was a wreck, with the mattresses pulled from the bed, and every drawer and door opened. Kotler's bag had been dumped, its contents spilled over the small desk. Kotler noted that the leather envelope that had housed the papers had indeed been opened, and the random sheets of notes he'd placed inside were all pulled out and oriented so they could be photographed. The leather envelope was off to the side, as if discarded. Which seemed odd.

Kotler turned to the open closet door and made a point of hiding the keypad with one hand as he punched in the combination with the other.

He had used a code he knew well—his nephew Alex's birthday. His encounter with Ricky had gotten him thinking about his brother, Alex's father. Maybe that was why he'd picked this particular sequence. Regardless, it was private, and Kotler didn't want to share it over this ridiculous premise that he might have murdered Ricky Miller.

The safe opened and Kotler stepped aside, allowing the officer to inspect its contents.

"Ok," the officer said, exasperated. "You could have told me there was nothing in here."

Kotler blinked and bent around the officer to peer into the safe. Denzel joined them. "Empty?" Kotler asked. "That's ... I put the papers in there before I left."

He turned and looked at the room, at the items on the table, and the pages of notes he'd left in the leather envelope. "Officer, when you and your team got here, what shape was the room in?"

The officer shook his head. "Kind of a mess. Blankets were on the floor. The desk was just like you see it. We've only been here a short while, but we've started picking through, photographing things."

Kotler shook his head. "That's not how I left the place. I hadn't been here long. Hadn't even had a chance to settle in. I left that envelope with my notes, sitting on the desk. That's it. The bed was made. My bag was there," he pointed. "And the papers were in this safe."

The officer eyed him, then shook his head. "Sure," he said. "Well, we have photographs. I'm sure Detective Kozak will share them with you later if you ask him." He smirked at this, and Kotler knew the Detective had already talked with his men about Kotler. They already had their opinions about him.

Denzel stepped into the room proper, holding up his

badge when the other two officers started to protest. "Someone was definitely looking for something, and knew you had it," he said, turning to Kotler. "How'd they get into that safe?"

Kotler shook his head. "It has to have some kind of master code." He looked at the officer. "You're going to need to talk to hotel management, and any staff on duty."

"Ya think?" the officer said, an ironic and malicious smile on his face. "I appreciate you telling me how to do my job. Now get out so we can finish up here, and don't leave. Stand outside the room."

"We'll be in the lobby," Denzel said squaring off with the officer before passing him.

"In the bar," Kotler added, following close behind.

IT WAS an hour later before Kotler was allowed back into his room. The police were interviewing hotel staff and management as Kotler and Denzel went upstairs. They entered to find Kotler's room in the same disarray as earlier. Denzel helped Kotler get things back in order.

"This won't be the last of it," Denzel said.

Kotler shook his head. "No. I'm sure Detective Kozak will swing around soon just to threaten me a little more."

"He's an ass," Denzel nodded. "But don't be too hard on him. He's doing his job. So are the officers who came in here. I think they're letting some personal bias bleed through, but so far it's only been words."

"So far," Kotler agreed, though he knew that words could easily influence actions. If Kozak and his men thought Kotler was guilty, they might not be quite as diligent in looking for the real killer and would be more biased to seeing evidence that damned him. That was a problem in more ways than one.

Once everything was put back in place, Kotler inspected his things. Nothing appeared to be missing. He hadn't traveled with much, to begin with—just a backpack with a change of clothes and some toiletries, all still intact. Even his smart tablet was still there. "I guess they figured I didn't have anything digitized that they'd need," Kotler said, motioning.

"Or they figured you could track the tablet," Denzel added.

Kotler nodded. That made sense, and it was true. But it opened up even more questions. Whoever had come in here was savvy enough to know how to deal with the safe, possibly having a master code or some device that would give them access. That indicated they'd been prepared to deal with the safe ahead of time.

Kotler thought back to the notes he'd stuffed into the leather envelope. They had been laid out side by side. Kotler had assumed that was so they could be photographed, but wouldn't it have been evident from the start that these were not the Spanish pages?

That hinted at something: Whoever had come here hadn't known precisely what they were looking for, or what it would look like. They had taken the time to set those pages side-by-side, in neat order, but had then turned the room over, looking for the real thing.

They were after the papers, specifically, and it didn't matter to them if Kotler had copies.

More than that, Kotler could now piece together the progression of events. The intruder had gained access to the room. The door had a modern lock, activated by passing a keycard over a plate in the doorframe. An induction system that could be fooled with the right technology, and enough determination. Still, that hinted at expensive resources beyond what the average person would have access to.

Access to the room. A quick scan of the documents in the leather envelope. Tossing the place to search for the real thing. And then access to the safe.

The sequence of events hinted at the intruder being a worker bee, not the Queen. They were following orders and making contact with someone on the outside. And all the while, Kotler had been taken out of play by an anonymous phone call, placing him at the scene of Ricky's murder and straining Kotler's alibi. It hinted at planning and distraction.

It hinted at an organization, not merely an individual, behind it all.

Denzel had just smoothed the blankets on Kotler's bed and had stepped into the bathroom, closing the door behind him.

Kotler glanced over and saw the leather envelope. He'd left it aside as they had cleaned up, placing the notes back in his bag. He picked it up now, absently looking it over as he thought.

He hadn't yet considered what he would do with it. His ruse hadn't worked, obviously. He had hoped that if anyone broke in here, they'd snag the envelope and retreat as quickly as they could, but whoever had broken in to steal the documents hadn't been fooled in the least. They'd gotten away with the papers anyway, despite Kotler's precautions. He felt slightly foolish about it but snapped out of it. What else could he have done, with such short notice? He had protected them as best he could, with the means he'd had available at the time.

There was the sound of a flush from the bathroom, and Denzel stepped out to the small vanity, running the water to wash his hands. Kotler was about to toss the leather envelope back onto the table when he noticed something.

Since Ricky handed this to him, Kotler had focused more on its contents than on the envelope itself. As he fanned it open just now, however, he realized that there was something etched into the interior—a pattern lightly burned into the inside of the material.

"Roland," he said, "could you hand me that small pair of scissors, from my toiletry bag?"

Denzel had just toweled his hands dry and gave him a strange look before sifting through the bag, producing a short, sharp pair of grooming scissors.

He handed these to Kotler, who used them to start snipping at the thick threads that bound the leather at its seams. The envelope was a continuous piece of leather, sewn along the sides, with a triangular flap that could be closed with a short leather thong.

As Kotler cut through the last of the threads along each side, he was able to lay the leather flat on the table, the inside facing up. He placed objects from the room on the four corners, to encourage the envelope to lie flat.

He stood back, along with Denzel, and under the light of the desk lamp, they could both see the etching more clearly.

"It's a map," Kotler whispered.

He took out his phone and shot several photos, getting close-ups where he thought the details might be obscured. The images were a high enough resolution that the extra shots might not be necessary, but he had a feeling this was going to become important later.

"What is it a map to?" Denzel asked, leaning in to inspect it closer.

Kotler shook his head but started picking up on details

as he studied it. In a moment, he felt he had a sense of the thing. Using his phone again, he made a few taps and swipes and then showed Denzel the result.

"I think it's a map of the Sonoran Desert. Or of part of it. The area just southeast of here," Kotler said. He zoomed in on the map. "It looks like most of this falls into the Sonoran Desert National Monument." He looked up to Denzel. "Federally protected land. A lot of that terrain is pretty rough."

Denzel looked closer. "What's this?" He indicated a mark on the landscape, and Kotler peered at it.

"I recognize that," Kotler said. He straightened and once again looked to his phone. He called up the photos Ricky had sent him, of the Spanish papers.

They weren't great photos. Taken in low light, and far enough away that they included random objects and tools on Ricky's workbench, the images were a little grainy and sometimes blurry. Kotler had been able to read some of the writing, but part of it had been difficult to fully interpret, until he'd seen the papers for himself. He wished he'd thought to take more photos, while the documents had been in his possession.

"Here," Kotler said, zooming in on one of the sketches.

He compared the drawing to the mark on the leather, rotating the image onscreen until it matched the map's orientation.

The mark resembled a rectangle, with four radiating, organic-looking hooks, almost like the arms of an octopus.

"Is that ..." Denzel started, then leaned closer before shaking his head.

"What?" Kotler asked.

Denzel squinted. "Maybe I'm just biased," he said. "Seeing something just because it's on my mind."

Kotler smiled. "Roland, what? What do you see?"

Denzel sighed. "Well, I just rewatched some of your TED Talk ..."

"Oh?" Kotler grinned.

"Don't get a big head about it," Denzel groused. "I was on the flight here, and it was on my phone. The in-flight WIFI wasn't working. I was bored."

Kotler chuckled but let it pass. "And what are you seeing now?"

"Well ... is it my imagination, or does that look a little like a swastika?"

Kotler's eyes widened in surprise, and he turned again to look at the symbol.

Denzel continued. "You said that before the Nazis starting using it, the swastika was a pretty common symbol, even with the Native Americans."

"I talked about the whirling log," Kotler whispered, nodding. "A Navajo symbol. But it does appear in a wide variety of native cultures. And yes, I think you might be right. This does resemble a swastika." Kotler straightened and thought for a moment. "The papers mention *División Azul*. A Nazi faction."

"Coincidence?" Denzel asked.

Kotler laughed. "About a month ago you asked me how many genuine coincidences we experience. No, I don't so. I think it's ... well, I think it's a code. Sort of."

"Code," Denzel said. "For what?"

"Well, if you wanted to indicate something important on a map, X would mark the spot, right? The swastika is kind of an X, isn't it? There are other symbols etched into this, but I think they may be markers. Or camouflage, maybe. Meant to distract us." He ran his fingers over the leather, at the spot where the Hohokam swastika was burned into the virtual terrain. "It looks like my uninvited guests were just as hasty about overlooking this envelope as I was."

"You think whoever broke in and stole those papers was really looking for this map?"

Kotler nodded. "I think they stole the key but left the map behind. I've already translated most of what was in those pages, just from a casual read. They were torn out of a journal, I think. Someone was documenting what they found here. But this," he pointed to the map. "This was what they were after. This is what got Ricky Miller killed."

Denzel thought that over. "You know that means we have to turn this over to Detective Kozak, right?"

Kotler nodded. "Somehow, I don't think this will do much to clear me, in his mind. But if it helps to find the real killers, I'm happy to hand it over."

"Killers?" Denzel asked. "Plural?"

"I don't think that whoever broke in here was working under their own initiative." He walked Denzel through the order of things, as Kotler had perceived them. "The timing of the call is suspicious as well. Whoever murdered Ricky did it just after I left, and then called the police. Maybe even while they were still in Ricky's house."

"But someone searched your place just after you left," Denzel said, nodding. "So two people."

"At least," Kotler said. "But I think it may go further than that. I think this hints at an organization."

"What kind of organization?" Denzel asked.

Kotler shook his head. "Not enough information yet."

Denzel huffed. "Alright then. Let's call Kozak and get this to him."

Kotler nodded and stood by as Denzel made the call.

He continued to study the map as Denzel spoke on the phone.

Whatever lay at that X—the Hohokam swastika—was the reason Ricky was murdered and Kotler was framed for it. Whoever took the papers would have to realize, sooner or later, that they'd missed something. They'd be back. Or they'd return to Ricky's house. If Kozak would listen to them, it might be possible to set a trap.

In his gut, however, Kotler didn't believe it would go that way.

He stared at the swastika on the map, and then looked at his phone, surveying the terrain using a satellite overhead of the region.

Something was there. And if Kotler could find it, he might be able to clear his name and take down Ricky's killer. But if things went wrong, Kozak could confiscate Kotler's phone and tablet—the only sources he had for the papers and this map, once they handed the envelope over.

Kotler stepped away from Denzel and quickly forwarded everything he had—photos, emails, and notes—to a secondary cloud storage he sometimes used with his virtual assistant. Gave the folder an innocuous name, and then deleted the sent message from his email app.

Whatever happened, Kotler intended to find that X on the map.

He just hoped he could stay out of jail long enough to get the chance.

6

"WELL, if it ain't Dr. *Too Good for the NYPD* Ludlum!"

Detective Pete Holden looked exactly as Ludlum remembered him, right down to the same rumpled suit and the same stained tie. He was just as portly as ever, too, and Ludlum eyed his paunch with a stern expression. "You're not getting enough exercise, Pete."

Holden scoffed at this. "I get plenty. I just ran down a guy half my age." He patted his belly with pride. "Table muscle. I got the fuel to keep going all day and all night." He laughed at this.

Liz shook her head but smiled at him. "Caught another bad guy without me? You're getting good at this."

Holden made a face. "Human trafficking. Can you believe it? Bad enough scum is out there killing folks, but selling kids as sex slaves? What kind of sick world is this?" He huffed and shook his head. "Anyway, you're not here for that, are you?"

Liz shook her head. "No. I'm here for a favor."

Holden regarded her, leaning back in his chair and

eyeing her along the line of his cheeks. He was studying her. Weighing her.

Holden was good at his job. One of the best Ludlum had ever worked with. He gave everything to it though, right down to his health and his happiness. She worried for him. But she couldn't change him if she tried.

"Favors aren't something I tend to like giving out, Liz. But for you? What do you need?"

"You had a case a couple of years ago. I helped, but I wasn't the lead on it."

"Which case?" Holden asked.

"Morgan Keller."

Holden made a noise, almost like a cough, with notes of disgust. Ludlum knew why. Keller's murder was still technically unsolved, though it was nearly a certainty that Gail McCarthy had been behind it. NYPD had it on its docket, but it was tied to an early Historic Crimes case, and the FBI's findings had ended up at least partially classified. The trail of evidence for Morgan's murder had dried up long before Gail had died, and the case was still a thorn in Holden's side.

"I can't give you access to an ongoing case. Unless you've got some orders from above?" He looked almost hopeful, raising an eyebrow as he said this.

"Are you telling me you want the FBI to take jurisdiction on this?" Ludlum asked, surprised.

Holden scowled. "Of course I don't. But it's sitting there like a bad meatball sub, giving me a stomach ache. I wouldn't turn away some help."

Ludlum considered this. "This may help a little. I need access to Baker Tait."

"The auction house?" Holden asked. "Where the victim worked? What for?"

Here was where Ludlum had to play things close, to be cautious. She couldn't give Holden the full story and couldn't share many details. The risk would be too high— someone was obviously staying alert to anything that might be an investigation into the origin of Historic Crimes. But Holden would need something. A reason to help her.

"I'm looking into something on my own time," she said. "Me and a friend in the Bureau. We're looking at a cold case, but we don't want it becoming public knowledge. It would ... complicate things."

Holden listened and nodded. "So you can't go in with FBI badges blazing," he said. "This is an unofficial investigation."

"Yes," Ludlum said. There was no point in lying.

"Alright. I could probably get us in there, set up some conversations. I can justify it under doing a follow-up on this. Tell me though, will I be wasting my time? You see any leads coming from this?"

Ludlum shook her head. "I can't say, because I don't know. I'm not sure our two cases are actually connected. There's just some overlap with Baker Tait."

Holden nodded again. "Liz, you know I've got a backlog of cases as it is. If I step away from any of them, I gotta have a good reason. Otherwise, I risk some scumbag getting away. You see what I'm saying?"

"I do," Ludlum said. "I wouldn't ask if it wasn't important. But it's up to you. I don't want to take you away from a more pressing case."

Holden shook his head. "No, that's not what I'm saying. I'm asking ... if I scratch your back on this, will your FBI buddy do me a solid in return?"

Ludlum raised an eyebrow. "I'm sure that can be arranged. Within limits."

Holden laughed. "Limits. Yeah, I got limits of my own. But mostly I just want to know I got a chip to call in if I need it."

"So no specific favors?" Ludlum frowned. "I can't commit my friend to anything."

"Last I checked, you work for the FBI, too," Holden grinned.

Ludlum laughed. "Ok, Pete. If you need anything, just ask. You always had that favor, though."

Holden stood and brushed some crumbs off of his coat. He shrugged. "I always feel a little better having all the cards on the table. So, when do you want to do this?"

Ludlum let out a breath. "How soon can you arrange it?"

Holden grinned. "Like that, is it? Ok. Give me an hour. I'll make some calls."

7

"TELL ME AGAIN," Detective Kozak said, leaning back in his desk chair. "Why didn't you give this to me from the start?"

Kotler sat on the other side of the detective's desk, surrounded by the rest of the bullpen. Men and women in police uniforms were bustling about, chatting or dealing with paperwork. Some were questioning witnesses or people filing complaints. Occasionally Kotler caught looks from some of the officers, making it plain they knew who he was.

Papers and files were stacked so high in front of Kozak that the man could barely be seen, but he had stubbornly refused to do more than settle back, forcing Kotler to have to sit forward on the edge of his chair to see who he was talking to. Kotler hadn't known Kozak long, but he suspected this was a tactic. Kozak struck him as the type of man who liked to keep everyone around him slightly on edge.

"I had no idea about the significance of the envelope. I

thought the papers were the important part. They still are, to some degree. They provide a key to ..."

"Dr. Kotler, I know you're used to lecturing people and pretty much running any which way you want, but right now you're the primary suspect in a murder investigation." Kozak had leaned forward now, his face fully visible over the stacks of papers. He was practically sneering. "So let's stop trying to run the show, right? I'll ask you questions, and you'll answer them honestly. I can have you thrown in a cell if I have to."

Kotler blinked and took a breath. His first impulse was to get angry and let Kozak have it. But it would only complicate things further, to antagonize the lead Detective. And though he wasn't sure there was any justifiable reason that he might be thrown in a cell right now, he wasn't as confident that Kozak might not trump something up. Being detained, at this point, would also complicate things.

Kotler sighed. "I'm not lecturing, I'm providing context. I believe that whoever killed Ricky was really after that map."

"And what makes you think that?" Kozak asked.

"A hunch, more than anything. But the map was hidden, and the papers were with it. Whoever broke into my hotel room knew I had this. I'm not sure how. I suspect they found out about it when Ricky bought the storage unit, where these were found."

"The storage unit," Kozak nodded. "I've had my people looking into that. Haven't turned up much so far. The lawyer who owned it wasn't local. He owned a piece of property south of Mesa. Remote. Probably a vacation home."

"I assume you've gotten a warrant to search the place?" Kotler asked.

Kozak gave him a hard look. "Don't worry, I know exactly how to do my job." He tapped the leather envelope, which now lay in an evidence bag on his desk. "You got any more bits of evidence you somehow forgot to tell me about?"

"I brought that to you the moment I found it," Kotler said. "Agent Denzel was there. He can tell you exactly what happened."

"And where is Agent Denzel?" Kozak asked, looking around symbolically.

"He had something else he needed to deal with," Kotler said. "He said you could call him if you needed to speak with him."

Kozak leaned forward, his neck bulging and a slight red tinge to his face. "Tell him this isn't an FBI case unless he's planning to make it one. I don't want to hear about him investigating this without running it through me."

"That's between you and the FBI. Tell him yourself," Kotler said. He was through playing polite. Kozak was trying to rattle him, and in part, it was working.

But it also felt personal. The man didn't like Kotler, that was clear. He seemed willing to pin Ricky's murder on him with even the flimsiest evidence. He'd gone out of his way to mention Kotler's wealth and position several times, so that was apparently an irritation for the Detective.

And Kozak's body language absolutely screamed his disdain for Kotler. He read like a man barely in control of himself. Or so he would have Kotler believe. It was possible he was putting on a show, bullying Kotler to keep him off balance. If he genuinely believed Kotler was guilty, Kozak was the sort of man who would use intimidation to the hilt.

Whatever the man's agenda, Kotler intended to play things straight when it came to Kozak. Any answers the

Detective wanted, within Kotler's power to answer, Kozak would get.

Kotler also intended to get answers of his own, independent of Kozak's investigation.

The police here hadn't exactly warmed to Kotler, and there was a chance they might be willing to look past evidence that would exonerate him, in favor of putting the out-of-town rich guy in prison. Kotler had seen this before—a sort of single-minded obsession with nailing not just the guilty but anyone who even *appeared* guilty. It was a wide-open door for corruption, and for putting an innocent man behind bars.

Kotler intended to make sure that was impossible.

With things wrapped up and the new evidence in Kozak's hands, Kotler left the building and retrieved his rental car. He started toward the rendezvous point that he and Denzel had agreed upon. As he pulled away and took a turn, he spotted a vehicle he recognized.

It was nondescript, particularly for the area. An older Toyota Corolla, somewhat beat up with a speckled paint job that hinted at its age and its exposure to extreme desert conditions.

There were hundreds of cars just like it, roaming the streets all around him. Kotler wouldn't have paid any attention to it at all, but he had noted the license plate back at the hotel. Though the plate was fully visible, it had a smudge of mud or grease or some other substance obscuring the number.

Kotler saw that smudge now, though the car itself had hung back by several lengths. It was following from almost a block back. Or seemed to be—it could just be a coincidence.

As a test, Kotler pulled into the parking lot of a convenience store and went inside. He stood at one of the turnstiles of sunglasses, near the glass door and the large store window, pretending to browse the selection. He glanced out to see the Corolla slowly pass.

Kotler decided to kill a few minutes. He bought a soda and a snack, as well as a pair of sunglasses—he hadn't actually brought any, and the sun here could be brutal. He paid, and then returned to the rental car. He sat for a moment, punching in an address into his phone's GPS, and then pulled slowly out onto the street, purposefully driving in the opposite direction from which he'd arrived.

He hadn't quite made it two full blocks before he spotted the Corolla behind him again.

The GPS alerted him that his turn was approaching.

Kotler had only recently renewed his driver's license, mostly at the insistence of Denzel, who had been appalled to learn that Kotler had let it lapse. As a consequence, the rules of the road were fresh in Kotler's mind, including the rules about using a turn signal at least 100 feet before turning.

He blatantly broke this rule, waiting until the street was nearly upon him and then quickly pumping his brakes before making the turn, with no signal.

Once around the corner, and obscured by some of the local homes, Kotler punched the gas, accelerating quickly. Up ahead was a four-way stop, and Kotler turned right once again, almost without slowing down.

The car following him had been a couple of blocks behind, and this maneuver had given Kotler enough of a lead to lose his tail. He could have kept up his speed and left his pursuer to wonder at where he'd gone. Instead, he pulled the rental to the curb, with an old pickup obscuring it, and then leapt out, sprinting so that he could stand on the sidewalk and watch the intersection with the truck blocking him.

In seconds the Corolla appeared and slowed, stopping at the four-way intersection. The driver was obviously looking for any sign of Kotler, and Kotler himself ducked behind the truck and peeked over its front hood.

A moment later the Corolla moved on, picking up speed as it went straight.

Kotler was back in the rental in an instant, and whipped around in the street, turning to follow the Corolla. Like his pursuer, Kotler would remain a couple of blocks behind, watching from a distance. He wanted to see where the driver went after giving up on finding his target.

But as Kotler turned onto the street, the Corolla was gone.

Kotler stopped, considering.

He didn't want to fall for his own trick. The driver must have turned into the neighborhood somewhere and might be watching for him to pass. This game might be a loop now, the hunter becoming the hunted becoming the hunter.

Kotler decided it was time to break the loop.

He turned around and had the GPS reroute, to make a wide birth around this neighborhood. He used voice to text to change where he and Denzel would meet up. As he drove, he kept flicking his eyes to the mirrors, looking for any sign of whoever had been following, but so far, the streets behind remained clear.

He wouldn't allow himself to start thinking of it as a coincidence. Someone was watching him, just as they had when Ricky was killed. But why?

They had the papers. So the only conclusion Kotler could come to was that they were after the map. Or, if they were unaware of the map itself, they were trying to see what else Kotler might have or might know. They might even intend to abduct Kotler—it was the sort of thing that happened to him, a little too frequently.

Handing the map over to Kozak should keep it safe, Kotler decided. Or, he hoped it would.

Right now he wasn't sure what was happening, or who to trust.

8

"What do you mean, someone was following you? Did you get their plate?" Denzel had done as Kotler instructed, and parked in an area behind the building where they could easily spot anyone else who arrived.

Kotler shook his head. "Not all of it. It was obscured. But I don't think it would matter. I suspect that car was stolen."

"You think this is the same person who called the police about you? Who searched your hotel room?"

"Could be," Kotler nodded.

Denzel considered this. "We should let Kozak know this is happening."

"For all I know, Kozak is behind it," Kotler said.

Denzel scoffed. "I seriously doubt that. I've looked into him and his department. Exemplary service. High honors. And a pretty high close rate. He's a jerk, but he's a good cop."

Kotler huffed. "I know. I'm just a little annoyed that I'm being investigated for Ricky's murder and being followed by the bad guys at the same time." He leaned against the hood of the rental car. "Did you find anything?"

Denzel nodded. "The attorney's name was Jim Messler. He retired about three years before he died. He lived in Houston, but he owned property in half the states, from what I could tell. Mostly real estate deals, income properties. He also owned properties outside the country. His place here seemed special, though. He was here half the year, with his son."

"So he has living family?"

Denzel shook his head. "His boy died. Pretty mysterious circumstances, too. He was here, staying at his father's place, and there was a gas leak. He never woke up. The questionable part was that there was a full inspection of the house and all the pipes and lines, just a month earlier. No leaks detected."

Kotler was surprised. "What about Messler himself? How'd he die?"

"Coroner's report says natural causes …"

Kotler caught the hesitation. "But?"

"He was being treated for low potassium levels. He had a prescription for potassium chloride. And the toxicology report showed his potassium was elevated slightly at the time of death."

Kotler nodded. "So they ruled it a cardiac arrest," he said.

"Except his prescription was empty, according to the investigator's report. They didn't make anything of it. Messler had a refill waiting at a local pharmacy. They figured he'd run out but was going to pick that up later."

"But you don't think it went down that way," Kotler said, shaking his head. "It's a pretty classic murder weapon since potassium would be released into the bloodstream anyway, during a heart attack. If he was already taking injections, the coroner might overlook any puncture marks. Where did they find the body?"

"In bed," Denzel said. "At his Houston home. It was a couple of days after he died. He was supposed to go on a hunting trip but never showed."

Kotler took all of this in. "What about his property? Kozak said he and his people were checking into the place."

"Bought up after Messler died," Denzel said. "A developer came in and bought a bunch of the local properties. Rumor is that they plan to build some kind of resort or something, but I haven't seen anything official. I have a call in to the county records office."

Kotler nodded. "I think someone was covering their tracks. Looking for those papers."

"Could be," Denzel said. "We can safely work from that assumption for now." He spread a folder open on the car's hood. "These are copies of the rental agreement where Messler had his storage unit. His name is on them, as the primary contact, but he was leasing it under a business name. That might explain why it wasn't found by whoever is looking for it."

"But when Ricky bought the unit, Messler's name became public somehow," Kotler said.

"I think so," Denzel nodded. "It seems like things got set in motion pretty quick at that point. Ricky reaches out to you, and you hop a flight here right away. A few hours later, Ricky's dead and you're being framed so the bad guys can search your room."

"Ricky said he reached out to me almost immediately, after going through the stuff from the storage unit," Kotler said. "Do you think they were tapped into his email?"

Denzel shook his head. "I don't think so," he said. "I

think they were making their way here, and you got here first. There might have been a lag in Ricky buying that unit and these people finding out about it. It just came down to timing. You organized and got on the move pretty fast. They may have had to make special arrangements."

Kotler absorbed this. It helped, actually, to realize that someone may have targeted Ricky before Kotler had even become involved. Kotler was still haunted by Ricky's death —he was a good man, and he didn't deserve this. But Kotler felt personally responsible for his death for the past day, and it was something of a relief to learn he wasn't culpable in any way.

Which did nothing to dampen his determination to find whoever did this.

"So what's next?" Kotler asked.

Denzel shook his head. "I'll keep digging on my end, but now that we know someone is tailing you, I think we should get you out of sight. Maybe find a safe house."

"I'm not going to sit in a safe house while all of this is happening," Kotler said, adamant. "The police think I'm a murderer, and the real killer may be trying to put an end to me. I'm starting to take that personally."

Denzel studied Kotler for a moment. "You have something in mind," he said.

Kotler grinned. "How can you tell?"

Denzel shook his head and shrugged. "You always have something in mind. So, spill. What kind of trouble are we about to dive into?"

9

Ludlum hadn't been back to the Baker Tait offices since she'd helped to case the scene of Morgan Keller's murder, nearly three years earlier. The place had changed quite a bit since then, with new furnishings and expanded warehouse space. The antiquities business, it seemed, was good.

Agent Dani Brown and Detective Holden stood on either side of Ludlum as they waited. Dani was hovering slightly behind, hanging back to remain discrete. Officially she wasn't there.

In fact, Ludlum herself was there only as a consultant— Holden had cleared her thanks to her prior role in the forensic investigation of Morgan Keller's murder, and Dani had signed off on it as the person currently in charge at Historic Crimes. The timing of this, with Denzel out of town, had been fortunate.

Bianca Miles, the General Manager of Baker Tait, stepped out of an elevator to greet the three of them. Holden made introductions, and when he got to Dani, he said, "This is Agent Brown, from the FBI. She's also consulting, though this is still an NYPD investigation."

He peered at Dani as he said this, and she made no sign that she was bothered by it in the least.

"FBI," Bianca said. "Do you happen to know Agent Roland Denzel?"

Dani and Ludlum exchanged a quick glance. "I do, actually," she replied.

"How is he?" Bianca asked. There was a hint of something in her voice, and Ludlum wasn't entirely sure what it meant.

Dani made a slight shrug and shook her head. "Good? He's out of town right now. I'm actually filling in for him."

Bianca smiled and nodded. "We ... went out. Once. Tell him I say hello."

Dani returned the smile and also nodded. "I'd be happy to share that message," she said, with perhaps a bit more enthusiasm than was warranted.

Holden stepped forward and started talking to Bianca, and Dani slipped in beside Ludlum. She mouthed the words, *Went out?*

Ludlum smiled but shook her head. She'd never heard any mention of it and wondered about it herself. Maybe when Denzel was back in town, she'd ask him about it, but she doubted he'd be very forthcoming with any details. Denzel was meticulously private about his personal life.

It occurred to her, then, that Kotler might know something.

Thinking of Kotler sent a tiny sort of panic through her. She hadn't heard from him since that text the other evening, but she knew that Agent Denzel had abruptly left for Mesa. The details of what was happening there were a little sketchy, but

Ludlum tried not to worry. She had plenty to keep her attention, between her official work at the FBI and this side project that was likely taking more of her time than it should have.

It remained to be seen whether this little field trip yielded any useful results, but it was a lead. It was low-hanging fruit, in a sense. The only immediate *in* they had with any of the auction houses on their list was here at Baker Tait. That made it a good enough place to start.

Bianca led them first to the elevator and then down a corridor to a small conference room. They were each offered coffee and tea and then took their seats. Holden removed his notebook from a coat pocket. "I'm sorry to say there hasn't been much progress in Ms. Kelly's case, and nothing I can share at the moment. But I wanted to circle around again, just to see if any new information may have come to light here."

Bianca sighed and shook her head. "No, I'm sorry. Really, it's sad, but the entire business has moved on since ... well, since the incident. I'm one of the few employees who was here when Morgan was around. Everyone else either left immediately after she died or has left since."

Holden made a note of this. "Other than you, who's left from that time?"

Bianca thought for a moment. "Some of the administrative staff have stayed around. We have new people come through all the time, but there are a few people in accounting who have been here almost since the beginning. And Andre, of course."

Holden checked his notes. "Andre Pierce?"

Bianca nodded. "He's part of our acquisitions team. Though he's more of a freelancer. He's worked with us for years, though, so I tend to think of him as part of the team."

Ludlum leaned forward slightly. "What does he do, as part of your acquisitions team?"

Bianca smiled. "I probably shouldn't call it a team. It's three people, two of whom are on staff full time, working here in the building. Andre is sort of a ... well, a field agent, for lack of a better term. We pay for his travel and accommodations, and he visits potential clients, to vet and verify what they have."

"Doesn't seem like that would keep him too busy," Holden said.

Bianca shook her head. "No, which is why we haven't hired him full-time. I know that he does work for other auction houses, and sometimes for independent clients. He sometimes takes jobs from collectors, who want him to negotiate a deal for them directly. It's sort of a conflict of interest, but we ignore it. My philosophy on it has evolved over the past few years, really. As long as he doesn't undercut us on any deals, or sell something out from under us, I don't see the harm. He does have to make a living, after all."

Holden flipped through some of the pages of his notebook. "I have notes from a conversation with him. Pretty brief, I guess. I don't have much from him."

Bianca nodded. "He wasn't here when Morgan was murdered. He was on an assignment elsewhere, I think. For a different auction house or maybe a private client, I can't recall. But when he got back to town, I had him reach out to you, just as you asked."

Ludlum glanced over Holden's shoulder. The interview notes with Andre Pierce were a short block of Holden's handwriting, on one tiny page. There was nothing that made them stand out.

Pierce had one of the best alibis anyone could imagine,

for Morgan Keller's death. He'd been at a viewing party in a billionaire's home and was recorded on video at nearly the exact time of the murder.

Ludlum could see why Holden would let that line of inquiry drop.

But something was tickling her brain about Andre Pierce.

"Could you give us any contact information you have for Mr. Pierce?" Ludlum asked.

Bianca nodded. "Of course. He's moved since the police last spoke with him. He lives here in Manhattan now."

Ludlum nodded and looked to Dani, who had sat quietly through the entire conversation.

The agent nodded when Ludlum looked back. Apparently, she'd gotten a vibe as well.

It was the mention that Pierce worked as a freelancer with other auction houses. Ludlum and Agent Brown happened to have a list of auction houses, and they would certainly check to see if his name could be linked to any of them.

Ludlum wasn't sure if this would bring any useful results, but it was a lead, and their first good one since this whole thing had started.

They wrapped up the conversation, and Holden thanked Bianca. "We appreciate your continued cooperation," he said.

Bianca shook her head and smiled. "I'm not sure my cooperation is doing much good, but I'm happy to help. Morgan was a friend as well as a co-worker. I miss her."

The meeting ended, and they took the elevator to the lobby. Once outside Holden asked, "You get what you needed?"

Ludlum and Dani exchanged glances, and both

shrugged. "We're further along than we were," Ludlum said. "Thank you."

Holden nodded, then climbed into his car and drove away.

"I'll run this guy's name when we get back," Dani said.

Ludlum huffed. "I have a backlog of work waiting for me, back at the lab. I need to get to it. Want to catch up again this evening?"

Dani nodded, and the two of them climbed into her car, heading back to FBI headquarters.

Ludlum rechecked her phone. Still no word from Kotler. Should she text him?

She decided he would reach out when he had time. Or when he thought about it. Maybe when he got around to it.

She knew she was being a little hard on him, but she also thought that maybe it was time to say something. It had been a few months since they'd decided they were officially some sort of couple—though Kotler had seemed reluctant to put a label on it. Ludlum had also been a little reluctant, for her own reasons. Kotler, for all his skills and strength and intelligence, could sometimes be a child, particularly when it came to personal commitments.

He had his reasons, she knew. And she understood. To a point.

She'd try texting him a little later, maybe after getting some work done. She didn't have to wait for him to come to her, she realized. Maybe he needed her to take charge a little and to step over his roadblocks and baggage. Maybe he needed her to come to him.

Maybe she needed that, too.

10

Turning off of Highway 8, into the Sonoran Desert National Monument, was like taking a right-turn into the old West. Hundreds of saguaro cactus spread across the terrain, and hills and mountains rose to envelop them. Denzel had rented them a more rugged vehicle for the trip —a Jeep with a soft top and rugged tires. They had loaded it with large cans of water, food, and camping supplies before trekking out in the early Arizona morning.

The road they were traveling went from paved to gravel to barely a road at all. This was where the Jeep earned its reputation, as the ground fell away into divots and gullies deep enough to get lost in. The ride was at times bone jarring.

The desert brush rose alongside the path now, obscuring their view and lending a sinister feeling to their journey.

Kotler and Denzel were already running at a heightened sense of impending danger, and the claustrophobic landscape along the road wasn't helping. The desert could be a dangerous place, they were both well aware.

Eventually, however, the horizon and the scenery finally cleared enough to reveal an immense pan of dusty desert expanse, dotted with drab-looking plant life and no sign of humanity, beyond the barely-usable road. In the distance, in all directions, the hills and mountains formed a bowl around them, under a vacant canvas of crystal blue sky and the blinding eye of the morning sun.

Aside from the GPS on their phones, which became less reliable in the absence of cellular towers, they'd brought along a few pieces of useful technology, including a dash-mounted GPS that Kotler had purchased and updated the evening before, programming it with their destination. He had ensured it had the most current and accurate maps of the Sonoran region as were available, and now they used the unit to home in on the location where the Hohokam swastika was leading them.

"How far out are we?" Denzel asked. He was driving while Kotler navigated and continued his research, looking over the photos of the Spanish papers and comparing them to the information he'd downloaded the evening before.

Kotler checked the GPS. "I'd say we're about fifteen miles out."

Denzel cursed. "At this pace, it'll be more than an hour before we get there."

"You're in a hurry?" Kotler asked, smirking.

"I'm not a fan of the road conditions. I don't see how you can read with all these bumps and potholes. I feel like my butt is six inches closer to my shoulders."

Kotler chuckled and closed his iPad, rubbing his eyes and then leaning forward slightly, stretching. "To tell the truth, it's tough. I'm feeling a little motion sickness, and my whole body hurts. Maybe we should pull over? Take a break and stretch our legs? We should still get to the site with plenty of daylight, and we can always set up camp nearby and get a fresh start in the morning."

Denzel nodded and pulled the jeep off of the road, cutting through the thin brush on the passenger side of the vehicle and stopping near a couple of tall cacti, providing slender paths of shade that were all but useless.

The temperatures weren't outrageous, thanks in part to it being early in the year. If anything, the morning air had been chilly until nearly 8 AM, and according to the weather reports it wouldn't rise above 74°F for several days. Comfortable weather, if a bit bright. Kotler was glad for the convenience store sunglasses.

Now parked, they exited the Jeep, and each stretched and moved, stomping the ground to loosen sore muscles. Denzel drifted to the back of the Jeep, opening the gate and rummaging for a bite to eat in his pack. Kotler sipped from a plastic bottle of water, and took his backpack out of the back seat, placing it on the ground in the shade. He knelt to inspect its contents.

Among the provisions, including his iPad and some research materials, was a small, handheld GPS unit that Kotler had purchased alongside the dash mounted version. This one resembled a walk-talkie but had a small alpha-numeric keypad, and a large SOS button mounted on its front, under the display. Here in the desert, where there were no cellular signals, a unit like this one was a lifeline. Not only could it be used for navigation, but it could be used to send an emergency signal and to communicate with the outside world.

Kotler had wanted a satellite phone, but they were sold out, and this was a good-enough alternative. It was a comfort, just having it.

Kotler had placed the unit back in his pack and was zipping things up when he heard the sound.

It was close. A pulsing thump that was deadened slightly by the flat and desolate terrain. But he recognized it immediately.

"Kotler!" Denzel shouted, pointing.

Kotler turned and saw a small helicopter rushing just above the tops of the saguaro, clearly angling toward them. It appeared to be a black Hughes 500—the type that police often used. This one was large enough to accommodate the pilot and three passengers, though from Kotler's vantage point he couldn't tell how many people were onboard.

The chopper slowed and banked slightly, and a figure leaned out of the open door. He twisted in his seat, braced a foot on the landing strut, and then leveled a rifle on them.

"Down!" Denzel shouted.

Kotler didn't need the warning. He knew instantly that he was caught out in the open, between the chopper and the Jeep, with barely anything beyond cactus and scrub brush for cover. He dove to the sand as shots impacted the soil around him.

Kotler covered his head with his hands, more as a gesture to protect himself from flying debris than from any delusion that he could deflect the deadly hail from above. The helicopter passed by, moving out of the line of fire, and Kotler looked up to make sure Denzel was alright.

Denzel had taken cover behind the Jeep and had drawn his weapon. He hadn't fired yet, and Kotler knew why. The shots would be wasted at that range, and it was better to conserve ammunition.

This fight was bound to get closer.

Kotler thought frantically. He hadn't brought a weapon

for a variety of reasons, not the least of which was that he was currently being investigated for murder. Just being out here, out of reach of Mesa PD, was pushing things enough. If he was caught with a gun, it might be enough of a spark to set off whatever powder keg Detective Kozak was packing for him. Right now, however, Kotler was kicking himself over the decision, and praying he lived long enough to feel foolish about it.

The helicopter was coming back around, angling so that the gunman could still have a shot. Kotler noticed then that men were approaching on the ground, from the direction the helicopter had come.

"Roland!" Kotler shouted, pointing.

Denzel was crouching now, and raised his weapon, firing at the men.

Kotler scrambled to his feet and sprinted toward the jeep as the man in the helicopter laid down more fire.

Kotler dove, taking cover behind one of the saguaros. Rifle rounds thunked into it, and in a moment, Kotler felt a sticky wetness splash down on him—water from within the cactus sprayed over him and the desert floor.

In another moment, Kotler felt a sudden attack of sharp pain over his buttocks and legs and realized that one of the limbs of the saguaro had been severed, dropping on top of him.

The helicopter passed once more, and Kotler got back to his feet, rolling the cactus off of him as gingerly as he dared. He limped away then, the pain searing but manageable.

Two men were ducked behind clumps of cactus and brush, engaged in a shootout with Denzel, who was holding his own, but just barely.

This was a bad situation, and Kotler wasn't entirely sure how they could get out of it. The helicopter was circling back around for another go at them, and it was clear the enemy had the better position.

Kotler looked frantically around the landscape and spotted an outcropping of stone.

"Roland! There!" He shouted and pointed, and Denzel looked up to see where he was indicating. Nodding, he ran for it. Kotler, still limping but pushing past the pain, also moved at a quick pace.

The gunfire ceased, but the helicopter's mad buzzing picked up again, indicating it was after them. Denzel got to the outcropping and turned, taking aim as Kotler hobbled forward at speed.

Shots were fired, and plumes of desert soil erupted skyward, causing a cloud of dust to rise around Kotler, some of it getting into his eyes.

Despite this, however, he got to the rocks and took cover just as more rounds pinged from the stone.

Denzel continued to fire, and at one point ejected the clip and inserted another one, pulled fresh from a front pocket of his pants.

"How many rounds do you have left?" Kotler asked.

"Ten," Denzel said, his teeth gritted.

Kotler nodded, and rolled back, huffing. He winced and reached back to yank a cactus spine free from the back of his thigh. It was covered in blood, and Kotler pondered for a moment whether it might be useful in any way. He was desperate for something—anything—that might get them out of this mess alive.

"Hey!" Denzel shouted, suddenly standing and taking a couple of shots.

Kotler also rose, looking over the rocks. The helicopter had banked once again, and was now moving toward the horizon, nose down and picking up speed.

That was a relief, but it was short-lived.

The two men who had approached on foot had gotten to the Jeep and were climbing inside. In a moment had it started and were racing away, bumping over the landscape in the same direction Denzel and Kotler had been moving.

Denzel let out a stream of curses, and Kotler silently joined him.

They had survived, which was good. But they were now stranded in the middle of the largest desert in North America, with no food, no water, and no vehicle.

Kotler settled with his back against the rock, looking up into the bright Arizona sky, and tried to take solace in the fact that his cheap sunglasses had never fallen from his face.

11

With the enemy gone, they slowly made their way from the rock, back to where the Jeep had been parked. The spot was a wreck of shredded cactus and churned earth, as well as spent shell casings. Denzel holstered his weapon and kicked at a clump of dirt, cursing once again.

Kotler shook his head. "Why didn't they kill us?" he asked.

Denzel made a noise. "Maybe they did. We're at least three day's walk from the nearest town. Being out here with no supplies, no water, we might as well be dead."

Kotler considered this, and his eyes widened. He raced to the spot where he'd been crouched, as the helicopter attack had begun. There, among the churn and debris, was his backpack.

He grabbed it and brought it to Denzel. "Small miracle," he said, "but I'll take it."

"Got anything we can use in there?" Denzel asked.

Kotler grinned. "Some water. Some food. Mostly things I needed for exploring the site we were headed to. But there's also this." He reached into the bag and took out the GPS unit.

Denzel sighed and nodded. "At least we can get a rescue," he said, relieved.

Kotler nodded. "But whoever took the Jeep is on their way to the swastika site," he replied. "The coordinates were plugged into the GPS. They know exactly how to get there."

Denzel shook his head. "Nothing we can do about that now, Kotler. First priority is to survive and get back to civilization, then we start working to find whoever did this."

Kotler was quiet for a moment, considering. "Roland ... it'd be dangerous, wouldn't it? To stay in the spot where the bad guys attacked us? It's our last known location. We should probably move on, maybe try to find help."

Denzel studied him and shook his head. "Kotler ..."

"For all we know there could be people nearby. Maybe in that direction," he waved vaguely in the direction they'd been moving.

"That's the problem," Denzel replied. "We *know* there are people in that direction. Armed people, with helicopters and the upper hand."

"Except they'd never expect us to come in over the ground," Kotler replied.

"Because it's just about the stupidest plan on Earth for two barely armed men to attack a fortified position."

"Unless those two men called for backup," Kotler said, holding the GPS unit up and wobbling it back and forth. "And we'd want to be able to give their exact position, wouldn't we?"

Denzel stared at him, then rolled his eyes. "How far was it?"

"Fifteen miles. Rough terrain, but we've hiked worse. At least we'd be moving."

"What about supplies?" Denzel asked.

"We'll divvy up what I have, but we can also make use of some of what's here. The cactus is edible, though we'll probably end up with diarrhea."

"And dehydration," Denzel said, shaking his head. "The pulp and water are too alkaline."

Kotler's eyes widened. "That's true!"

"Don't act so surprised, Kotler. I was Special Forces. I did have just a teeny bit of survival training."

Kotler chuckled. "I'm suggesting we could eat the cactus as a last resort, though I don't think it would come to that. I have some charcoal tablets in my pack, which will help. I also have a water filter. One of those portable pumps." He looked around and spotted what he was hoping for.

At the base of one of the saguaros was a husk, the remnants of another cactus, long dead and dried. He picked it up and turned it to shake any loose debris from it. "Saguaro boot," he said, showing it to Denzel. "Natives used these like canteens. If we can find a source of water, we can filter it and store it in here. Worst case, we might be able to filter the cactus water enough that it won't make us sick."

Denzel nodded. "Ok. But if we call for help, they're going to want us to stay put."

"We wait," Kotler nodded. "But we wait at the swastika site and call for help there. We can use the GPS to send a text to explain what's happening, to make sure any help they send is armed and prepared. We hit the SOS and leave it stashed, so they have a signal to follow."

Denzel closed his eyes and shook his head. "I can't

believe I'm going to go along with this. It's the dumbest plan I've ever heard."

"Whatever these people are after," Kotler replied, "it can't be good for anyone. Right now we're the only people close enough to have a chance to stop them. And if we find them, we can bring in reinforcements. I don't think this is a terrible plan. Just not a ... comfortable plan."

"Meaning we're going to be pretty miserable by the time all is said and done, especially if we aren't rescued by nightfall. Ever been in the desert at night, at this time of year, with nothing but the clothes on your back?"

"Actually, I have," Kotler said. "And worse. So have you. It's not fun, but we survive. It's what we do. But it's fifteen miles on a cool day. We can make that, easy."

Denzel nodded at this. "Alright, let's not waste any more daylight. We'll get moving. But first," he stooped and started gathering shell casings. "Never know when something like this might come in handy," he said, shoving them into his pocket.

On that note, Kotler scoured the ground for anything else that might be useful. He found his water bottle, which he had dropped during the attack. It was empty, but it still had its uses. He shoved it into his pack. He also removed a packet of spare shoelaces he'd purchased, made from paracord. He used these to fashion a harness for the saguaro boot, securing it to his pack.

They were all set for water-carrying vessels. If only they had water beyond the spare bottle in his bag.

Having scavenged everything they could use, the two of them set off in the general direction they'd been moving earlier. Kotler periodically checked the GPS, to ensure they were on track.

"I still have my phone," he said to Denzel. "It was in my

pocket when we were attacked. I've shut it off to conserve battery, but it might come in useful. I have pretty much all of the research backed up on it."

"Comforting," Denzel grunted as he stepped over a large stone. "At least we'll have something to read."

Kotler chuckled at that, and let it pass. Denzel was playing grumpy, and likely was genuinely put out by all of this, but he was also onboard with the plan and the reasons behind it. This was a crazy trek to undertake, but Kotler felt it was necessary, and he knew Denzel trusted his judgment.

As they walked, they spoke very little, conserving both energy and water. As a result of the silence, as well as the monotonous landscape and the hypnotic rhythm of movement, Kotler began to think about things he'd managed to keep at bay for days now.

Mostly he thought about Liz.

He needed to reach out to her. He should have called her, or at least sent a text, before they'd left. He'd meant to. But he'd put it off. There had been a slight tinge of dread about it, and Kotler had allowed himself to procrastinate.

He wasn't sure why.

Since that kiss, months ago, Kotler and Liz had taken things slow but steady. They'd gone out several times, had spent hours chatting and taking walks through Manhattan, touring museum exhibits and taking in shows. Softer dating, as Kotler thought of it. Safe. Maybe even timid.

In the past, Kotler's relationships had been more ... dynamic. Most hadn't been serious in any way, but those that were had been intense, filled with emotion. And sometimes filled with danger and betrayal, when he considered Gail McCarthy.

His relationship with Gail was mostly a ruse on her part. She had arranged for the two of them to become involved, in an attempt to enlist Kotler's help in a takeover of her grandfather's vast smuggling empire, wresting control from her "uncle," her grandfather's partner. Kotler had inadvertently given her exactly what she'd wanted, effectively raising her to the status of an international threat. She'd been on the radar of law enforcement agencies around the world, and it had eventually fallen to Kotler to take her out.

He was still dealing with that. Even with her gone, Gail was still influencing him.

Even before Gail, though, there was Evelyn Horelica—a linguistics expert who ran in the same scientific circles as Kotler. The two of them had dated for quite some time, and their relationship had been passionate and exciting. But it had also been limited, and that was on Kotler. She wanted more than just a tryst, more than stealing moments of passion between conversations about their work. She had, in truth, wanted Kotler to settle down. And that had scared Kotler to death.

He could admit, now, that he had sabotaged their relationship even while relying on it for some sort of vicarious stability. He had loved Evelyn, but he had also used her. He had kept their relationship going but hadn't done a thing to move it forward. Ultimately it was this, even more than Evelyn's abduction by a crazed billionaire, that had led to the collapse of even their friendship. Things had really started ending well before her abduction. And they hadn't spoken in more than a year now. There'd been maybe a couple of emails in all that time—both devoid of any emotion. It was over.

With Gail, things had been different. Kotler felt no pressure from Gail, no push to take things to the next level. Now he knew why, of course. It was by design. Everything about their relationship, about Gail herself, had been a complete fabrication. She had fooled him and taken advantage of him.

She had loved him, too, as far as Kotler could tell. In her own way. In the way that only a true sociopath could love someone. A way that led to Kotler's life, and the lives of everyone he cared about, being in constant jeopardy.

So Kotler had become, quite literally, a bit gun shy about relationships. He was understandably hesitant about getting into another serious one, especially so soon. And for her part, Liz appeared to understand this and even accept it.

To a point.

Kotler wasn't an idiot. He could read body language better than nearly anyone, and he knew the ins and outs of human psychology pretty well. He could see the signs. Liz loved him and was being incredibly patient with him, but she was getting tired of waiting, and he couldn't blame her.

Kotler could read the signs in himself as well.

He knew that he was running.

He'd been running since the start, and he wasn't sure if he could stop.

He had to try, though. Liz was precisely the sort of person he knew he should be with—brilliant, kind, honest. He needed to make things right with her.

Or he needed to end it.

There was no grey area here, Kotler knew. He had to decide whether or not he really was ready for this relationship, and from there he needed to make one decision or another. Either he was all in, or he was all out. He owed that to Liz, and to himself.

The problem was, as clear as his introspective analysis could be, he still wasn't sure what was really going on in his own heart and mind. He knew he was allowing his experience with Gail to cloud everything. But he wasn't sure why, or how to resolve it.

He just needed time.

Well, he thought, *you have 15 miles of desert to cover, with not much more than your thoughts to keep you entertained. That might be a good amount of time.*

They marched on.

THE TERRAIN HAD SLOWED them to a near crawl at times, but on the whole, both Kotler and Denzel agreed that they likely made the best possible progress. At least the cooler weather kept the rattlesnakes at bay, possibly hibernating or curled under the rocks, conserving warmth. They steered clear of any spot that looked like it might conceal danger, just in case.

The only other wildlife they'd seen were a few birds circling in the sky. Thankfully they weren't buzzards, though the image was close enough to put both men in a contemplative mood.

The dry, cool air had made things comfortable enough as they marched, though they were both dehydrated. Kotler split the water with Denzel, dividing it into the plastic water bottle he'd saved. He had discarded the saguaro boot when it became obvious that they wouldn't find any water on the path. They could find another easily enough, so there was no sense lugging it around. Though he did retrieve the paracord laces.

Now they crouched behind a pile of rocks at a distance from the location the map had given them. Looking down the hillside, they could see both the helicopter and the Jeep parked at the foot of a mountain.

"Time to call it," Denzel said. "Hit the button."

Kotler nodded and shrugged off his pack. He had the GPS hanging from a length of repurposed paracord around his neck, and he looped this up and over his head. He tapped out a message using the small keyboard, giving as much detail as he could, identifying himself and Agent Denzel and asking for backup at their location. He then hit the SOS button and dangled the GPS by the paracord like a hypnotist's watch.

"Done," he said. "We can monitor for any response. But I think we should stash this somewhere."

"Why not keep it with you?" Denzel said.

"Just in case we get caught."

Denzel eyed him and shook his head. "You want to go in there," he said. "You want to go into the mountains and track those men."

"I at least want to get to the Jeep and see if there's any water left," Kotler replied, holding up his near-empty water bottle. "And we might be able to get it back. Or even get the helicopter going. Taking away their air support might be good. You can fly one of those, right?"

Denzel rolled his eyes. He looked over the edge. "I don't see anyone guarding the place." He slid back down next to Kotler and shook his head. "That doesn't make much sense."

"Maybe they're shorthanded," Kotler said. He studied the mountains and the vehicles, then took his phone out of the front pocket of his jeans.

"There's not going to be a signal out here," Denzel said.

Kotler shook his head. "I'm looking at the photos of the map." He powered up the phone and brought up the map and studied it, comparing features to their location. It was a reasonably precise depiction of the region, and Kotler could quickly pick out landmarks.

He had no idea who had drawn it. He assumed it was members of the Spanish Blue Division who had obviously been here during World War II. The swastika had to have been some clever decision on their part—an ironic way to mark the map with something local but meaningful to them. So it made sense.

But what about the other symbols on the map?

Kotler had studied this since they'd found it, and he'd considered several possibilities. The symbols might have been camouflage, masking the swastika's presence so that anyone who discovered the map might not recognize it right away. That made a bit of logical sense, and it was the assumption that Kotler and Denzel were operating on.

But what if these other symbols indicated something else as well? They might be camouflage, but couldn't they also be notations? Guideposts meant to point out something else that the Blue Division might have needed to note?

Kotler was about to comment on this when Denzel once again peered over the edge. "I think we should at least get to the Jeep. Some of our provisions may be in there, like you said. And I have a spare weapon and ammunition in my pack, if it's still in the back of the Jeep."

"A spare?" Kotler asked, grinning.

"You have a bad habit of needing a gun," Denzel said.

Kotler chuckled. "Case in point." He tucked his phone away, the question of the other symbols momentarily forgotten. He joined Denzel in eyeing the spot below.

It was true, there was no sign of anyone. There was a hint of a trail or path, an open spot that led into the hills. It was obscured by an outcropping of rock. It must have been the route the bad guys had taken.

"Ok, what's our plan?"

Denzel shrugged. "Not much to it. We follow the line of

the hill, stay low, and make our way to the Jeep. It should provide some cover, once we're close enough. If they left the keys, it'd be a miracle. But I can hotwire it if I need to."

"It's nearly dark," Kotler said. "But we should move now." He motioned to the Western hills, where the sun was already descending, and the last rays of daylight were cast in hues of red. "The shadows should obscure us well enough, but we'll still need some light. We shouldn't risk flashlights."

"Do you actually have flashlights?" Denzel asked.

Kotler shrugged. "I have my phone. So yes. But I also have a small tactical light in my backpack. Part of my exploration kit."

Denzel shook his head and rolled his eyes. "Of course you do. Alright, let's move."

Kotler paused only long enough to hang the GPS off of a small ledge of rock, obscuring it with bits of debris and brush from nearby. The two of them then started their crawl down the hillside.

It was strenuous and slow going, but they made good progress. As they moved, both Denzel and Kotler would occasionally rise from their half-crawl, half-crouch to see if there was any sign of the men who had attacked them. So far things looked clear.

At the bottom of the hill, they were only twenty feet or so from the Jeep. Denzel checked and readied his weapon, quietly moving the slide to make sure he had a round chambered. He looked at Kotler. "You good?"

Kotler nodded.

"I'll move for the driver's door. You come up behind. The passenger side is in view of that path, so don't run for the seat until I give the all clear. They could be watching from somewhere in that direction."

They moved then, Denzel running in a crouch with his weapon raised. Kotler lagged by only a few paces.

As Denzel approached the driver's side of the Jeep, he put a hand on the door handle and looked over his shoulder to Kotler, giving a nod.

Kotler picked up the pace, keeping low but moving quickly.

Denzel pulled the handle, and the Jeep's door opened.

The interior light came on.

Kotler had almost made it to the back of the Jeep when a shot was fired from the mountainside above them, followed quickly by another.

"Cover!" Denzel shouted, crouching down behind the Jeep's door, his weapon raised, scanning the hillside.

Kotler ran now, full tilt, and heard two more shots before he reached the back of the Jeep. One had been so close he'd felt it disturb the air.

He was breathing heavily, more from adrenaline and fear than from the exertion of running. He heard the sound of the Jeep's door thunk closed and glanced over the spare tire on the back of the Jeep to see that Denzel had climbed inside. Seconds later he heard the engine start even as two more shots struck the Jeep's hood.

Kotler pulled the handle on the Jeep's tailgate, swinging it wide and diving inside just as Denzel punched the gas. The tailgate bounced outward as Kotler held on to anything he could find. Looking out he saw dust rise in twin clouds, illuminated red from the taillights in the growing darkness.

More shots were fired, and there was a sound like a small explosion, followed by cursing.

"There went one of the tires!" Denzel shouted back to him. "And I think they got the engine!"

The Jeep was sputtering, and Kotler looked forward,

seeing steam rising in jets from the two bullet holes in the hood.

More shots from above and Denzel turned sharply, putting the passenger side of the jeep between them and the shooter, just in time for the engine to die altogether.

Denzel rolled out of the driver's side. "You see my pack back there?"

Kotler had been so concerned with taking cover he hadn't noticed, but as he looked, he saw Denzel's bag. He rummaged through it and found the spare gun and the clips.

He crawled out of the Jeep now, staying low, and ducking under the tailgate of the Jeep. He tossed one of the clips to Denzel and shoved the other into his weapon, chambering a round.

"This is not going well," Kotler said.

Denzel peeked over the hood of the Jeep. The gunman, hidden in the darkened hills, was taking only occasional shots now.

"He's just holding us here," Denzel said. "They'll come for us. We'll have to make our stand here and hope our signal got through. How long do you think it would take them to get here?"

"If they have air power, and think to use it, maybe thirty minutes," Kotler responded. "Could be a few hours if they come by ground. The terrain is pretty rough out here."

"I remember," Denzel said. He peeked over the Jeep again. "Visibility is getting low." He cursed. "We should have stayed put. This was a bad call."

"It's on me, Roland," Kotler said.

Denzel shook his head but said nothing.

Kotler raised his weapon and glanced around the tailgate. It was already quite dark here at the foot of the hills. The Jeep was their only source of light, casting sharp rectangles onto the ground a few feet out. Visibility was low, and the light from the Jeep wouldn't provide much of a heads up if someone were approaching. Worse, it was shining like a beacon, telling the enemy exactly where they were.

"We should cut the lights," Kotler said.

Denzel nodded, and reached into the Jeep, turning the key off and throwing them into darkness.

Things went quiet then. Not a good sign.

There was a sound from behind them, but before either of them could turn a voice said, "Put your weapons on the ground and your hands on the back of your heads."

Denzel and Kotler turned only enough to see that two armed men were standing behind them, weapons raised.

Doing as they were told, Denzel and Kotler lowered their weapons and raised their hands. One of the men came forward, taking the two handguns and Kotler's pack.

"You must be Dr. Kotler," the other man said. "Well, that's a surprise. You saved me an ass chewing for leaving you out in the desert."

"Oh good," Kotler said. "I love being helpful."

"You'll be helpful," the man replied. "We need you inside."

With that, the men forced Denzel and Kotler to stand and then shoved them roughly ahead, into the darkened path that rose into the mountain before them.

12

"THAT'S HIM," Dani said, leaning over to whisper. Though the noise of the bar made whispering redundant.

Ludlum and Dani were dressed to the nines, each wearing their best little black dress. They had colorful cocktails in front of them, but they were nursing them slowly. The drinks were camouflage. They both planned to stay sharp.

Ludlum didn't look immediately, but after a beat, she turned as if scanning the room.

"Black shirt, ponytail, beard," Dani said from behind her.

Ludlum spotted him right away, and let her gaze wander past as if she were looking for someone in the bar.

Andre Pierce was with friends, drinking and dancing, enjoying the night. He didn't look the way Ludlum had imagined him, but he did look rich. Very rich.

"I was expecting someone older," Ludlum said, turning back to the bar.

"Me too, at first," Dani replied. "Turns out he got a

pretty early start in this business. He has a sealed record, from when he was sixteen, but otherwise, nothing to indicate any criminal history. He brokered his first deal by the time he was 18, for a pair of 17th Century cufflinks that belonged to William Penn. I couldn't find any information on the seller, but the buyer was Dr. Lester Rodham."

"Rodham ..." Ludlum frowned. "That name sounds familiar."

Dani nodded. "It should. He was questioned in Morgan Keller's murder. He does a lot of business with Baker Tait. Or did, before our boys harassed him and took one of his toys."

"He was the one who had the other stone," Ludlum nodded. "The Edison stone. The one that matched the artifact owned by Gail McCarthy's grandfather."

"Yeah, the file gets a little fuzzy around that point," Dani said. "There's some deeply classified stuff in there. I have no idea why they were after those stones."

Ludlum shook her head. "Doesn't matter. So Andre worked with Lester Rodham. More than once?"

"Years," Dani replied. "It wouldn't surprise me to learn that half of that guy's collection came in through Andre, funneled through Baker Tait. Though I think the other half came in through Richard Van Burren."

"That was Edward McCarthy's partner?"

"Right," Dani nodded. "He also funneled these things through Baker Tait. Those guys get a lot of Rodham's business."

Ludlum thought for a moment, then shook her head. "Why?" she asked.

"Why what?" Dani replied, confused.

"Why would Andre Pierce funnel the things he

procured through Baker Tait? Bianca Miles told us they knew Andre was a freelancer. They were fine with it, as long as he didn't snake any deals away from them. Going through them instead of going directly to the buyer must have cost him a cut of the sale. So was he just keeping things on the up and up? Making sure he didn't lose a good client?"

"From what I can tell, it was Rodham who connected Andre to Baker Tait in the first place. And maybe to a few other auction houses around the world."

Ludlum thought about this. "Do you think Rodham was trying to get a man on the inside?"

Dani smiled. "That's exactly what I think."

"So Andre may actually be our link," Ludlum nodded, glancing over her shoulder. Andre had started dancing with one of the girls from his table, the two of them grinding to an obscene beat from overhead. Ludlum turned back to Dani. "Why are we here?"

"I was thinking we might talk to him," Dani replied. "If we can get him away from his date."

"I think he has too many people with him to really make this work," Ludlum said. "He's preoccupied."

Dani nodded. "It was a gamble. I followed him here from his apartment. Which is pretty posh, by the way. He almost lives like your boyfriend."

Ludlum made a face at the mention of her "boyfriend." Kotler hadn't called, hadn't so much as sent a text, and it was really starting to irk her. She had been glad to get Dani's text, telling her to pull on a dress and get here as quickly as possible. She needed the distraction. She needed anything to keep her from texting first.

"So what now?" Ludlum asked.

Dani shook her head. "I'm out of ideas. Running all this after-hours limits what I can do without bringing a lot of trouble down on us."

Ludlum thought for a moment. "What if I posed as a buyer?"

Dani considered this. "I think that could work. What are you buying, though?"

Ludlum shook her head. "No idea. Yet." She thought for a moment and then took her phone out to do a quick search. It took a bit, but she finally found what she was looking for. She held up a photo. "Dan sent this to me a few days ago, asking my opinion."

On her phone was an image of a figurine, a rough effigy of a man carved in stone. Kotler had been interested in it because, as he put it, the man looked as if he were wearing a space suit—or the ancient equivalent to one. Ludlum had to agree that there was some resemblance.

Kotler had told her the item had come up for sale by a private owner. He hadn't said how he'd learned about it, but Ludlum did know it wasn't a public offer. Kotler wanted to know what she thought about it, and explained he was on the fence about buying it. "I'm not sure I buy into the ancient aliens thing," he wrote. "But this would just be an interesting part of my collection. Something to look into later. Maybe something I could donate to an exhibit."

Ludlum had said that it seemed like the sort of thing he'd like—an interesting enigma for him to dig into.

She wasn't certain, but it felt to her like Kotler was trying to connect with her by sending her the image. Maybe he wanted to see if she was interested.

She had been, too. She asked questions and wanted to know more about it. She wasn't sure it was an ancient astronaut either, but she suspected Kotler wasn't altogether hung up on that idea. It was just a way for the two of them to connect over something he was interested in, Ludlum believed. It was Kotler making an effort. And it was the sort of effort that kept her hopeful about the two of them.

Kotler was bad about going radio silent, but he did try.

"A fat guy in a suit?" Dani asked.

"That's as good a guess as any," Ludlum smiled. "I have some information on the seller. I could approach Andre and say I was referred to him."

"Referred by who?" Dani asked.

Ludlum shrugged. "Maybe Rodham?"

Dani eyed her, shaking her head. "I'm not sure that's a good idea. Rodham has been laying low since whatever happened with the Edison stone. I looked into him. He's got some pull in the political arena. After his encounter with Agent Denzel a few years ago he became a little more reclusive, hiding out in an abbey he owns in Vermont. He quietly supports various political figures, but otherwise doesn't get much press. There isn't much on him. No way to know for sure what relationship he has with Pierce these days."

"Do we know if he's still getting merchandise through Baker Tait?" Ludlum asked.

Dani shrugged. "Not really, but from what I've read about the guy he's pretty into his collection. So we might assume."

Ludlum thought this through, then nodded. "Ok, it's a gamble. But I think it's maybe our best shot."

Dani huffed. "Alright, I'll back that. Just be careful."

Ludlum stood. "Wish me luck."

Dani raised a drink to her as Ludlum made her way across the floor, dodging through the crowd until she stood close to Andre and his girlfriend.

"Andre Pierce?" she asked.

Andre was still gyrating but looked at her side-glance. "Do I know you?"

Ludlum smiled and shook her head. "No. I … I represent a collector. Someone who would appreciate your help in procuring an item."

The girl dancing with Andre seemed to be oblivious to the conversation, and he put his hands on her waist, gave her a long and lustful kiss, and whispered something in her ear. She smiled and dropped into the booth with the rest of their friends, and Andre motioned for Ludlum to follow.

Ludlum glanced at Dani, who was already repositioning herself, making sure she had them in sight.

They came to a table in the far back of the club. Andre picked up a couple of empty glasses and put them on the thin ledge that ran along the wall. He used a couple of cocktail napkins to sweep the surface of the table, soaking up a couple of condensation rings, and then tucked the napkins into one of the empty glasses. He gestured, smiling, and Ludlum took a seat.

"It's not often I get approached about my work out in public," he said. "So this must be a … special case."

Ludlum smiled and nodded. "My client is interested in possibly having a long-term relationship," she said. "But first he wants to see how things go." She took out her phone and showed him the figurine. "This item is up for sale by a private owner. Nothing too … difficult."

Andre looked at the image and laughed. "That's it? I could have that for him by morning."

Ludlum nodded. "That'd be a good start."

"Who is your client?" Andre asked.

Ludlum let her eyebrows arch. "We hardly know each other, Mr. Pierce. That's more of a fifth or sixth date sort of question."

Andre laughed. "Fair enough. I have plenty of clients who like to keep things on the down low. But I do have one requirement. I need to know who referred you to me."

Ludlum nodded. Time to make her play. "Lester Rodham," she said.

Andre looked surprised. "Dr. Rodham?" He shook his head. "I haven't done much business with him lately. I heard he's involved in something. How is he?"

"Involved in something," Ludlum repeated, smiling.

Andre laughed. "Fair enough. Alright, any friend of Rodham's is a friend of mine. He basically gave me a start in this business. So I'm taking it that if I work out this deal for your client, then there could be more deals in the future? Things they may not want anyone knowing about?"

"That's the idea," Ludlum said. "Do you do work that stays off the books?"

Andre laughed. "You ... could say that. And I work with all the big auction houses worldwide. Helps me keep things legit, so I can cover the off-book stuff. Your client wants something smuggled into the US."

Ludlum recognized immediately that she was supposed to be impressed by his deduction, and she played along, trying to look surprised and maybe a little suspicious. "How did you know?"

Andre smirked. "It's my business to know. Alright, this is an easy enough trial run. If your client can pay my fee, I'm in. And then we'll talk about the other stuff, once I see how this goes."

"What's your fee?" Ludlum asked.

"Twenty percent," he replied. "Plus expenses."

She nodded. "Alright. You said you can get it to me tomorrow?"

"How's 9 AM sound?"

Ludlum smiled. "Sounds like we're off to a good start."

AS HE'D PROMISED, Andre arrived at 9 AM sharp with the statue in hand, nestled into a foam insert in a small metal case. He placed the case on the café table in front him and popped the two clasps, opening the lid and turning the case with a flourish.

Ludlum inspected it, and took photos of it, pretending to send them via text to her "client." In reality, she was texting Dani, who was back at FBI headquarters writing off-the-cuff responses that occasionally forced Ludlum to suppress a laugh.

Her phone chimed with Dani's latest and Ludlum studied the screen, nodding. "Ok, looks like we have a deal."

Andre smiled and handed her a card. "That's the account and routing number where you'll wire the money. The total is written on there as well. I'll get a notice when the payment has gone through."

Ludlum looked at the card and forced herself not to cringe at the number. She worried for a moment that it might be more than she had access to. Again she took a photo and sent it to Dani. She then arranged to wire the funds to Andre, pulling from her personal savings. She'd have to figure out a way to replace that money later, but for now, they needed to earn Andre's trust.

Still ... she felt her face go warm and a trickle of sweat roll down her side.

Andre smiled. "Good, I see it. Alright, then. Did I pass?"

"With flying colors," Ludlum smiled.

"So what is it your client is looking for that he can't get through regular channels?"

"I can get you details when I have them. But he's looking for a way to legitimize this, so that if it comes out that he has it, he won't be suspected of anything. I'm told you can take care of that?"

Andre studied her for a moment, then nodded. "It's a little tricky, and it slows things down. But I can filter the item through a legitimate auction house. It will add to the price, but it has its advantages. Insurance, for a start. If the item is ever confiscated, the insurance will compensate for it."

"And what keeps anyone from learning that the item is for sale through auction?" Ludlum asked.

Andre shook his head. "It isn't an auction. The auction house will operate as a private broker for the deal. They'll insure it, perform inspections, and secure its delivery. I'll bring the item to the auction house, complete with authentication papers, and they'll provide it to your client."

"You can fake authentication papers?" Ludlum asked.

"Who said anything about fake?" Andre smiled. "Don't worry. I've done this thousands of times for my own clients, including Dr. Rodham. Everything is documented and legit by the time it gets to you."

Ludlum nodded and took the information Andre gave her, making arrangements to speak with him again in a few days. She needed time to find an item for him to bring in.

He's in, she texted Dani as Andre left her at the café.

Good, Dani replied. *I think I have just the item for him to procure. And now I can officially bring some FBI resources into play.*

Ludlum smiled, making her way to an Uber waiting a couple of blocks over. She was carrying the case with the figurine and clutched it like it might fly away. It represented a significant investment on her part—and not just financially.

Maybe she'd tell Kotler she got it for him as a gift.

Maybe he'd help her buy groceries for a few months.

13

THEY FOLLOWED the steep path into a gap in the mountain face, and after a time they came to a leveled spot at the mouth of a cave. One of the men pushing them forward had a tactical light on his weapon and used this to light their way. As they moved deeper into the rising stone, they eventually emerged into a gap in the mountain, a natural amphitheater open to the night sky above.

The space was roughly circular, and the rock face of what must have once been an enclosed cave curved upward from the floor, creating overhangs above them. Battery-powered lanterns had been set up in strategic locations here, illuminating hundreds of paintings and etchings in the cave walls. From this spot, more tunnel openings in the stone led to paths going in dozens of directions, radiating outward from the center like spokes on a wheel.

Two more men were standing nearly in the center of the space. One was holding the papers that Ricky Miller had given to Kotler just a couple of days earlier.

Kotler felt tense with anger at the thought of Ricky's murder but breathed through it. He needed to remain calm, to find out what these men wanted. Above all, he needed to stall them long enough for help to arrive.

"Dr. Kotler." The man holding the Spanish papers moved toward him. He held the papers up, rapping them with his knuckles. "I'm not sure how you did it. We found nothing in these to point to this cave system, but you did. Very well done."

Kotler decided not to mention the map. There might still be something useful there, and he preferred to keep any useful bits to himself—and away from these men—for as long as possible.

The men had taken his phone when they searched him, but it was locked, and Kotler had no intention of ever unlocking it, even if they tortured him or Denzel. Though he hoped it wouldn't come to that.

He glanced at the papers in the man's hand and froze.

The man had his sleeves rolled up, despite the chill of the night, and on his forearm, Kotler saw a tattoo of a symbol he recognized—the *Croix pattée*. The footed cross that many associated with the Knights Templar. But this was a specially arranged form of the cross, and it was one that Kotler had seen before.

The design included two concentric rings, filled with radiating triangles, almost like a starburst or a child's drawing of the sun. Within these circles was a set of four chevrons, their points meeting in the center to form the cross.

Kotler had seen this symbol many times, but one of the most memorable had been within the past year, while on a trip to Colorado.

"The Knights of Jani," Kotler said, his eyes locked on the tattoo.

The man paused, then held up his arm as if inspecting it

for the first time. He smiled and nodded. "You've heard of the order?"

Kotler had not only heard of it he'd been abducted by one of the leaders of the order. He'd been enlisted—albeit against his will—to solve the riddle of the Jani sigil and allow the order to regain access to their hidden temple and treasure vault, tucked away in Cheyenne Mountain.

The trouble was, there had been two factions of Jani, bent on gaining access to that vault. One faction, led by a man calling himself Granger, was benevolent, even if their methods were a bit rough. The other, led by a man named Talon, was an offshoot from the older organization and had plans for world domination. Plans they would have enacted using the very historical treasures the Knights of Jani had sworn to protect.

"I've ... worked with some of your people in the past," Kotler said. He couldn't be sure which faction he was dealing with here, and since they were enemies by blood, it would be dangerous to align himself one way or the other. He would need to play this close to the vest.

The man studied him, then nodded. "My name is Scope."

"Scope?" Denzel scoffed. "What kind of name is Scope?"

Scope smiled and shook his head once. "It was my call sign. I'll let you figure out why."

With a sudden move that was so quick Kotler wasn't sure he'd even seen it, Scope punched Denzel in the jaw, using the flat of his palm.

Denzel fell back, sprawling on the ground, and the other three men in the room chuckled. The two men who had forced them into this amphitheater bent and dragged Denzel to his feet.

Denzel rubbed his jaw with one hand. "Point taken," he mumbled.

Scope smirked and nodded, then turned back to Kotler. "So you got us this far, Dr. Kotler. I'm really glad we didn't kill you, because now we have no idea which way to go. I don't want us spending days in this cave. You're going to figure it out for us."

Kotler understood instantly that this wasn't a request.

Scope handed him the Spanish papers, and Kotler took them closer to one of the lanterns, lifting and angling it to see them better.

He'd studied these papers from the blurred photos that Ricky had sent via email, but it was infinitely better to have his hands on the real thing again. Kotler quickly read through the handwritten account again, and looked closely at the sketches, trying to make connections between the documents and the symbols spread out on the walls before him.

There were several Hohokam symbols meticulously drawn and detailed on the pages. The trouble was, none of the sketches seemed to correspond to the handwritten notes on the pages, nor to any of the symbols on the walls surrounding him.

The pages seemed to be ripped from someone's personal field journal—notes kept for their own research. The mention of the *División Azul* was the only real hint Kotler had about the purpose of these pages, or of the map. But beyond that, useful information was scarce.

Kotler remembered the words of his first mentor, Cristoff Vellar—his father's research and business partner, and the man who had taken in Kotler and Jeffrey after their parents died.

When there appears to be no path forward, reconsider what you already know.

Even as a child Kotler had realized the wisdom of the idea, though it had taken some time to make a habit of it. And now, examining the Spanish papers under lantern light, he purposefully calmed his mind and thought back on what he already knew, starting with *División Azul*.

The Blue Division had been Hitler's frontline force on the Eastern front during World War II. The primary task of the division was to rout the Russians and impede the advance of the Red Army while the German forces sliced up and occupied the territories formerly protected under the Molotov-Ribbentrop Pact. This had been the non-aggression treaty between Stalin and Hitler, and it was thrown out the window barely two years after the signing, hurling the Soviet Union into the war with Germany without the benefit of being on good terms with the Allies.

So much for good-faith deals with Nazis.

Despite this, the Spanish had thrown in with Germany at least as far as agreeing to fight on the Eastern front, not only pushing back against Red Army advancement but glee-fully slaughtering as many communists as they could manage. The *División Azul* was both a scalpel and a hammer —an elite force that Hitler had been impressed by enough to give the entire division its own unique award for service. They were tactical and efficient, but they kept to the Eastern front, to avoid conflict with their neighbors among the Allies.

It made little sense to think of the Blue Division even being on US soil, so far from the front, except ...

Hitler had a penchant for items of the occult and of ancient civilizations, particularly any item that hinted at the existence of a master race. He coveted anything that might provide some sort of arcane advantage over his enemies. Power and purity were Hitler's obsession, and he'd sent factions all over the globe in search of artifacts and written histories that might provide either clues about an ancient and lost culture, or the secret to replicating that culture's advanced power or technology.

There were numerous verified accounts of a Nazi presence in South and Central America, both before and during World War II, and it certainly would be no stretch to imagine Nazi operatives making their way to Arizona.

It would have been far easier, particularly as the war waged on, if those operatives were native Spanish speakers, even if they spoke a slightly different dialect from the Hispanic population of the Americas.

Could it be that Hitler recruited operatives from the Blue Division and sent them on a quest to research and retrieve any artifacts that might help Germany to defeat the Allies?

Kotler felt it was safe enough to assume this was the case. And at any rate, here he was holding a document that strongly hinted at the scenario. But how did all of this tie into the existence of this network of tunnels?

He looked up from the papers to study the symbols at each of the tunnel entrances.

In all, he counted thirteen entrances, radiating like spokes on a wagon wheel, away from the central cavern. One of those spokes was the path they'd used to enter, so at least he could eliminate that.

He stood and moved closer to one of the remaining entrances, holding the lantern up to cast light on the stone. There were etchings and paintings on nearly the entire surface of this cave system. This had obviously been a sacred place. But Kotler was surprised to find that not all symbols were Hohokam. There were symbols here that might have come from a variety of Native American tribes. But there were also symbols that he recognized from far more ancient sources—the Aztec and the Maya, among others.

He looked back to the papers. The symbols drawn there were primarily Hohokam, but now he saw the anomalies standing out like blazes in the night. "Rocket ship," he whispered, smiling and laughing to himself.

The rocket symbol that had gotten Ricky's attention was the most obvious. Kotler had struggled to reconcile that symbol with anything he could find from the Hohokam. But now, considering it in the lantern light, he realized that it wasn't Hohokam at all. It was from a different culture. It could have been Mayan or Aztec, but either way, it was clearly from an outside source.

What did that tell him? How could he use that information?

"Dr. Kotler," Scope said from behind him.

Kotler glanced back, raising a hand, placating. "My apologies, I'm trying to put this together."

"I wouldn't take too long," Scope smiled. He was standing menacingly close to Denzel, who had his hands in his pockets, looking oddly casual under the circumstances.

Kotler nodded and turned back to the papers and the cave walls. He moved from entrance to entrance, aware that the four Jani in the room were watching closely, ready to shoot him if he attempted to run. He ignored them and continued his survey of the tunnels and their associated marks.

The problem became obvious then. None of the symbols on these pages matched any symbols he could find on the walls.

Artwork covered literally every surface here, but Kotler picked out a pattern at each cave entrance. On the pillars of stone to the right of each opening, he found that there were always groups of four symbols in proximity to each other. They were obscured by the rest of the artwork, but Kotler spotted that these symbols were always etched and painted, rather than simply painted on the surface of the wall. He ran his fingers over the symbols on the column closest to him.

There were four symbols, with each group signifying some form of information about the tunnel it represented. The number four had significance with many Native American cultures, in much the way that the number three had cultural relevance among Europeans. It was a number that signified strength and stability—such as the four legs of the deer or the buffalo.

That was interesting and notable. It helped Kotler to confirm that these four symbols, at each tunnel entrance, were the notations that mattered most. They were the symbols he needed to pay attention to, in order to decide which tunnel to take.

The challenge was that Kotler was missing the key to decoding that information, and it was making it difficult to solve this. It was a bit like seeing that there is writing on a page, recognizing it as language, but being unable to read that language and glean anything useful from it. Deciphering this was taking time.

Though he had to admit, he was also dragging his feet just a little.

There was a familiar sound from the sky above, echoing down into the amphitheater formed by the open roof of the cave. Kotler looked up to see Scope signal one of his men, who promptly raced down the exit tunnel.

Kotler exchanged a look with Denzel, who nodded as if trying to direct Kotler's attention downward. Kotler looked and saw Denzel flex his hand within the pocket of his pants. He looked back up, and Denzel nodded.

He had a plan.

Kotler had no idea what Denzel had in mind, but he knew he had to be ready. He glanced around quickly and moved himself to a position beside one of the tunnel entrances. This one curved as it moved deeper into the mountain. It may or may not be the right tunnel to lead them to whatever Scope and the Jani were after, but it should provide some cover in a firefight.

He glanced back to Denzel, who again nodded, understanding.

Kotler gripped the lantern and the pages.

Scope's man came racing back in. "We're under attack! There are two helicopters out there, and they've already put an armed unit on the ground."

Scope nodded and turned to the other two men. "Take up positions. You," he said, pointing, "keep an eye on the roof. They may try to come over that lip. You two, move into that tunnel and take out anyone who comes through. We'll have reinforcements of our own soon." The men scattered, with two running down the corridor and the third taking a position opposite of the tunnel entrance, eyeing the ridge above.

Reinforcements. Kotler didn't like the sound of that, but he couldn't think of any way to let the police outside know.

He would have to come up with something later because Denzel suddenly took his hand out of his pocket and threw a glittering cloud of spent shell casings into Scope's face.

The Jani leader shouted, raising a hand to cover himself,

and Denzel slammed into him, paying him back for his earlier punch with two hard and fast punches to the man's jaw. He grabbed Scope's weapon and rifled through the man's shirt pocket to remove something else Kotler couldn't see.

The Jani watching the opening above them turned his weapon on Denzel, but hesitated, not wanting to risk hitting Scope's prone form. Denzel took advantage of the hesitation and raced to the tunnel where Kotler was already moving ahead. Bullets ricocheted from the stone floor and walls as Denzel sprinted forward, rounding the curve and nearly slamming into Kotler.

It was then that a cacophony of gunfire started. Kotler wasn't sure if any was being directed their way now—the noise was deafening, and he lost all sense of where it could be coming from.

"Where does this lead?" Denzel asked.

"No idea," Kotler replied. "Away from the fight!"

"Move!" Denzel shouted, and the two of them sprinted into the darkness with the lantern's light guiding them.

14

Ludlum and Dani stood outside of the interview room, watching a monitor upon which Andre Pierce was sitting at the plain table, leaning forward on his elbows and staring down at his hands. Not for the first time, Ludlum wished she had Kotler's ability to read body language. She'd love to know more about what Andre Pierce was thinking right at that moment. Though she had a pretty good idea.

The sting had gone off perfectly. Dani had set up a handoff, leveraging an item that was on loan from the New-York Historical Society—part of a traveling exhibit that was being packed for the next leg of its journey. The exhibit had given some legitimate context to the scenario and helped to keep Pierce from suspecting their trap.

Ludlum had acted as a go-between, but as soon as it was confirmed that Pierce was ready to make the exchange Dani and a team of agents descended on him like Valkyries.

He'd been cooling in the interview room for just over an hour.

"Ready?" Dani asked.

Ludlum nodded, and they entered the room.

There was no question that Pierce recognized Ludlum the moment she entered. He nearly flinched just seeing her, and his expression darkened momentarily before settling back into a picture of fear and misery and regret.

"Mr. Pierce," Dani said, showing her badge. "I'm Agent Danielle Brown. This is Dr. Elizabeth Ludlum." She motioned to Liz, who lifted her ID hanging from a lanyard around her neck. "We'd like to ask you a few questions."

"Entrapment," Pierce said. "This is entrapment."

"We received information indicating that you are often involved in the procurement of historical items on behalf of your clients, and that sometimes these items have been obtained through less than legal means."

Pierce said nothing but was back to looking down at his hands.

"Mr. Pierce," Dani said, "you're in a lot of trouble. But there could be a way out for you."

Pierce glanced up, hope finally coming to his eyes. "How?"

Dani paused for a moment, letting the tension build. "We're not after you. Not exactly. We have some questions about your dealings, some of your clientele. But mostly we want to know more about how you move the items you obtain."

She produced the list of auction houses they had obtained from the man in the park. "We've done some digging. Looks like you've worked pretty closely with every auction house on this list."

Pierce inspected the list and nodded. "Yeah, almost all of these are clients of mine."

"And you often represent individual clients in negotiations for items obtained by these houses?" Dani asked.

Pierce said nothing.

"Mr. Pierce, we know that you sometimes arrange for clients to procure items from these places, and that sometimes those items have been obtained in ... well, let's just say a 'less than legal' way." She put another document on the table. "This is a list of items reported stolen by their owners over just the past six years. These all somehow found their way to these auction houses, with legitimate papers verifying their authenticity. Some of these were sold before you started your work in this business. A lot of them were sold after, though. And those all have you in common. So what we'd like to know is, how are these items being obtained and authenticated? Who are you working with?"

Pierce glanced from the documents to Dani and then to Ludlum. "I ..."

He hesitated, and Ludlum could see he was on the verge of panic.

She exchanged a look with Dani, who nodded.

"Andre," Ludlum said, her voice soft and soothing. She leaned forward, her hands on the table. "Like Agent Brown said, we aren't after you. There's something bigger going on. Something that we believe is putting a lot of people in danger. Including ... someone I really care about."

Pierce watched her as she spoke, and gave a slight nod, glancing down. "I don't know any names. They just reach out to me when they need to move something, or I reach out to them when I have a client looking for something in particular. We have a system. Messages on a forum, online. Look, I'm really nothing, ok? I make arrangements between these guys and the auction houses. I'm a go-between. I let them know what a client is looking for, and they clean it."

"Clean it?" Dani asked.

"They give it papers. I don't really know how they do it. They just make sure that all of the records at the auction houses show it's legitimate and authenticated. They did it with this thing that you busted me for." He waved vaguely to the distance.

Ludlum nodded. "But you don't know how they do it? Or who they are?"

Pierce shook his head, staring at his hands once again.

The questioning went on like this for almost two hours, with very little progress. Dani arranged for Pierce to be taken to a holding cell, and she and Ludlum met in Denzel's office to discuss what little they had learned.

"It's not a total bust," Dani said. "We know how he reaches out to whoever this is."

Ludlum sighed. Pierce had been more than willing to give them everything on his channel of access to the people behind the scenes. But she knew that odds were that if they'd gotten any wind of Pierce's arrest, they were already moving on.

"This has been going on for a very long time," Ludlum said. "Decades. Some of these cases are from before Andre was born."

"So there are more people like Andre out there," Dani said, nodding.

"And whoever is behind this is also smart enough to have stayed off of the FBI's radar for decades."

Dani considered this and shook her head. "What I'm not seeing yet is the connection to Historic Crimes. Our contact in Central Park hinted that this was how we'd dig that up. I think I have more questions now than when we started."

"New questions, at least," Ludlum said. "Probably a good sign. But what now?"

Dani shrugged. "We keep looking. We'll use what

Pierce gave us, track it back as far as we can, and see what else crawls out from under whatever rocks we turn over."

"What can I do to help with that?"

Dani sighed. "Nothing. Not at the moment. It's not exactly a dead end, but it's kind of a narrow alley."

Ludlum understood. They'd put a lot of hope on this bust, and the payoff hadn't been as big as either of them had anticipated. Now, Ludlum would have to go back to doing whatever digging she could, in her spare time.

"Hey," Dani said. "We did get some leads from this. Don't look so glum. If nothing else, we now have a legitimate FBI case associated with this. I can allocate some resources to it now. It's progress."

Ludlum smiled and nodded, and then left Dani to get to it.

She returned to her lab and spent the rest of the day going through her own caseload, looking over results and writing reports. She hadn't exactly been absent over the past few weeks —she'd kept up with everything. But suddenly she felt like she had loads of extra time. She still felt that itch, to dig deeper and to keep looking for answers. But with nowhere to direct that at the moment, she turned it to getting ahead on other things. Eventually, she came to a stopping point. She closed her laptop and stood, stretching, letting her stiff muscles loosen.

Wrapping up for the day, Ludlum stowed her laptop in her grandfather's medical bag and took a cab home. Once back in her place she changed into workout clothes and went downstairs, jogging to the park a few blocks away, prepared to do a full circuit to blow off some steam.

It was edging toward night, but there were plenty of lights and lots of people around. There were carts selling hot dogs and gyros at the head of the trail, and the smell of grilled onions reminded her that dinner should be in her future. But first, the run.

She sprinted through the trails while listening to music from her phone, tuned out and but not quite oblivious as she moved. She let the rhythm guide her, becoming hypnotic as the pounding of her feet and the expansion and contraction of her lungs fell in sync with the tune in her ears. Her mind wandered. And then, suddenly, she became sharply focused.

She saw him up ahead, standing at the edge of the path, and recognized him immediately.

He didn't look at her, but he seemed aware that she was close, and that she had spotted him. He turned and walked away from the running path, toward a set of benches by the water.

Ludlum slowed to a walk, huffing from the exertion of her run, and stuffed the wireless earbuds back into their charger as she followed him. She was on full alert now, cautious and eyeing everyone around her. There are plenty of people around, but no one seemed to be watching her. Which, of course, did not mean that they weren't.

She came to the bench where he was seated and eased down next to him, forcing herself to breathe normally.

The last time she'd seen him, the man was dressed almost exactly as he was now, standing at the entrance of a tunnel in Central Park. He had handed her the thumb drive then—the same thumb drive that Ludlum and Dani had used to find the case files and to track down Andre Pierce.

"You're making some progress," the man said.

Ludlum didn't look directly at him. She was still glancing around to make sure this wasn't some sort of trap. "Yes," she said. "A little."

"The files I gave you came in handy then," he nodded.

"Yes. But ... where did those come from? What's the connection with them and Historic Crimes?"

The man chuckled. "Well, that's supposed to be the part you're figuring out."

"So you don't know?" Ludlum asked.

"I know some things. But nothing that would really be all that helpful, unless you and Agent Brown discovered it on your own. You have an official FBI case now."

Ludlum considered this and shook her head. "Are you saying that was the point? You gave us leads so we could get an official case open?"

"You two were sniffing around and starting to get noticed," the man replied. "You needed an official reason to look into these things. Now you have one."

Ludlum thought for a moment. "So you're saying that this thing with Andre Pierce may not lead directly to the answers we're after, but it gives us a legitimate reason to look into things that will."

"It was the best I could arrange," the man replied. "But it puts you much closer."

"Ok," Ludlum nodded. "Is there anything else you can give us? Anything that might speed this up?"

"You're in a hurry?" the man smiled.

"When we first met, you told me that all of this was about Dan Kotler. But some of the cases you gave us go way back. He would have been a kid when some of those artifacts were moved."

"Is there a question in there somewhere?" the man asked.

"Is Dan in danger? Is ... whatever this is ... is this investigation going to be dangerous for him?"

"In some ways," the man replied. "Dan has always been prone to being in danger. Even when he was a kid. But no, he's not in immediate danger. At least, not from this. You have time. You might want to use it, and not rush. If you push too hard, the people behind the scenes for this may take notice and take action."

Ludlum thought about this. "Ok," she said. "What about the FBI investigation? Is that in any danger of pushing too hard?"

"Not entirely," the man said. "The trail that you and Agent Brown are on will give you something to use as cover."

"Cover," Ludlum repeated. "It's a smokescreen? This is related to Historic Crimes, but not directly?"

"It's an excuse to look into things that would otherwise be red flags," the man said. He brushed his knees and then stood. "I'm going to walk that way," he said, pointing along the waterline to a set of buildings surrounding a parking lot. "You go the other way."

Ludlum stood as well, and squared off with the man, blocking him. "What's your name?"

The man studied her and shook his head. "I told you before that I can't reveal that. It puts me and others in danger."

"I have to call you something," Ludlum said.

The man considered this and smiled. "Call me DB."

"DB?" Ludlum asked. "What does it stand for?"

"Deep Background," the man smiled. "It means a source you can never reveal officially. How's that?"

Ludlum considered, then nodded. "Ok. DB. It'd be really nice if I had a way to get in touch with you."

"You have no reason to get in touch with me," DB said. "I can't answer most of your questions anyway, and when you do need something, I'll show up to provide it."

"Maybe I should call you Deus Ex then," Ludlum said, half joking.

He laughed. "That's a good one. But no, I think God would take some offense to any implication that I was playing his role in all this. DB will do just fine. Now, back to your run, Dr. Ludlum. Must stay fit."

He turned to leave, then paused, facing her again. "I almost forgot." He reached into the inside of his coat and produced an envelope. He handed it to Ludlum.

"What's this?" she asked.

"Balancing the books," DB said.

Ludlum opened the envelope, and her eyes went wide. Inside was cash—a stack of hundreds. She quickly counted and realized it was the exact amount she'd pulled from savings, to pay for the artifact she'd bought off of Andre Pierce.

"Tell Dan to enjoy the figurine," DB said. "Though perhaps you should leave out how you got it."

He wandered away then, and Ludlum watched until he disappeared behind one of the buildings. Cars were moving in and out of the parking lot, and it was dark enough that she couldn't be sure if he were in any one of them. She assumed that he was.

She shoved the envelope into the waistband of her workout clothes, then started her run again. Rather than continue on, however, she jogged back to her place. She dropped the envelope onto the table, near her grandfather's bag, so she wouldn't forget it. She wasn't sure yet what she would do with it. She'd work that out in the morning.

She made her way to the bathroom, peeled off her workout clothes and showered. After dressing in her night clothes, she made a meal. Calm. Normal. Keeping everything rhythmic, just as she had with her run. She let all the new questions settle into that place in her mind, where she made a mental note to follow up on clues and to start making connections. Just like she did with her forensic investigations, she was letting the details have time to coalesce.

She sent a text to Dani after she'd had time to decompress and think things through.

I'll give you more details in the morning, she said. *But I'd like to be assigned as the forensic lead on the Andre Pierce case.*

Dani responded a moment later. *You're already on it. What prompted you to ask?*

Tomorrow, Ludlum replied. *Tonight I'm going to have at least one night of Netflix and ice cream.*

Understood, Dani replied. Then, a few minutes later. *You ok? You need company?*

Ludlum considered this, and responded, *No, thanks anyway. I'd rather have some alone time tonight.*

Except this was a lie.

She would have loved company at that moment—someone she could tell this to, and someone to be a sounding board for her questions and ideas. She really could have used someone who would listen to her spill this whole thing out as verbal puzzle pieces, and help her start sorting them and fitting things together.

It was just that Dani wasn't the one Ludlum most wanted to see.

She thought about Kotler, now somewhere out in the desert with Agent Denzel. It was a fair bet that he was in trouble again, just like DB implied. She would have loved just to get him on the phone for five minutes, but she knew that wasn't likely. He'd have no mobile coverage out there, for a start. But beyond that, he seemed to be hesitant lately.

Something that had irritated her at first, but was now starting to worry her, for more than just their relationship.

DB had said something that nagged at her.

Dan has always been prone to being in danger. Even when he was a kid.

It was a familiar thing to say about Kotler, and it made Ludlum realize that DB must know him. And in fact, must have known him for a very long time. He must have been a part of Kotler's life, possibly since Kotler was a little boy.

That realization made her feel all the more worried and afraid, for some reason. And she would have given anything to hear from Kotler at that moment.

She sent him a text. *Just checking in. How is everything going? I miss you.*

It felt a little pathetic, but she was past caring about that. Lately, she'd come to realize things were happening in the world that she knew next to nothing about. And as DB had told her in their first meeting, it all came back to Kotler.

She prayed he was ok.

15

KOTLER AND DENZEL were in trouble.

They raced along the tunnel with no real clue as to where it would lead—a dangerous place to find themselves. They could easily find themselves at a dead end, sitting ducks for the Jani if any of them came this way. Their biggest hope was that the four men from the amphitheater were too engaged with Arizona police to pursue them.

But Scope had said *reinforcements*.

"We have to find a way to get a message to the police outside," Kotler huffed as they moved along. "Scope said other Jani are coming. These guys tend to be well armed."

"Any ideas?" Denzel asked. "Does this tunnel lead out, maybe?"

Kotler shook his head. There was no way to know. He'd chosen this passage at random, simply because he'd been standing next to it when things went down. He still had the papers, though they provided very little help. At least the lantern was coming in handy.

They pressed on, rounding a right turn that lead them,

by Kotler's estimate, on a generally westward course. A few hundred paces further and the passage turned right again.

"Wait," Kotler said, slowing.

Denzel paused with him, raising his weapon to cover the passage behind them.

"There's something ..." Kotler trailed off, thinking. "Dammit, I wish I had the map."

Denzel glanced at him, then patted his chest pocket. He tossed something Kotler's way.

Kotler caught it, though his hands were full. He fumbled a little, trying to keep it from going to the ground. When he'd settled and could look to see what it was, he smiled.

"You grabbed my phone?"

Denzel shrugged. "It was in Scope's pocket, just sitting there. I didn't want them to have access to anything that might be on it. And I figure you have stuff in there we might need."

"Roland, when this is over, I'm buying you dinner."

"Steak," Denzel said.

"As big as your head," Kotler laughed.

He powered up the phone and unlocked it, bringing up the map with a swipe.

"Any sign of trouble coming?" Kotler asked.

He and Denzel listened, and Denzel finally shook his head, relaxing a little. "I think we're good for a minute. What's going on?"

"I think I just clicked to something about the map." He held his phone up to Denzel. "See these other symbols? I thought at first they might just be camouflage. Zebra stripes, meant to hide what the map is really revealing."

"What are they?" Denzel asked.

"I think they actually represent these tunnels," Kotler

said. "Look at this one. If you picture the amphitheater and the tunnel that brought us in here, this symbol lines up with it. See the shape? A snake? That tunnel was long and had only a few slight bends."

Denzel nodded. "And this one has had a couple of hard rights," he said.

"Exactly." Kotler slid the map over and zoomed in on a square symbol consisting of right angles. "This is us," he said. He thought for a moment. "This was one of the four symbols carved into the stone, just at this tunnel's entrance."

"So what does that mean? Can you tell where it's going to take us?"

"No," Kotler said, shaking his head. "Not really."

"So we could be running for a dead end," Denzel replied.

Kotler only nodded.

"Well, let's get to it then. Better than being gunned down back in the amphitheater."

Kotler could only agree, and at that the two of them raced along once again, taking turn after turn. The bends were coming at shorter intervals now, and Kotler estimated they would get to the center soon.

And then they reached it, abruptly, and stopped short.

Ahead, reflecting back at them in a dull, reddish tone, was a stone wall.

A dead end.

They stopped, huffing, and Denzel immediately took a position that would give him some cover as well as a sight-line down the last leg of the tunnel. "Now what?" Denzel asked.

"I was about to ask you the same thing," Kotler replied.

Denzel shook his head. "We could probably hold this

position for a long time, but without provisions or supplies or extra ammo, it's going to be a short stay anyway." He settled in, his back against the stone wall, his weapon ready.

Kotler turned, scanning the space where they'd found themselves, hoping he could figure something out from here.

He had already rolled the papers, storing them in a Velcro-sealed pocket on one leg of his pants. He slipped his phone into his hip pocket to free up at least one hand while he used the other to sweep the light of the lantern over the stone walls. He stepped forward, running his fingers over the texture of the stone, studying it carefully to spot something—anything—that might be a way out for them.

"These are carved walls," Kotler said, surprised. "That's incredible."

"Must have taken years," Denzel said.

Kotler nodded. "And going by the number of tunnel entrances we saw in the amphitheater, there must be nearly a dozen of these."

"How can that be, though?" Denzel asked. "I mean, I know we're in a mountain, but some of those tunnels seemed to head back in the same general direction as the entrance. Wouldn't they eventually come up against the outer edge of the mountain?"

"Probably more dead ends," Kotler said. "But at least one of those tunnels has to lead to whatever the Jani are after."

Denzel studied Kotler for a moment, then slid to the ground, the gun resting against his knee. "What's the story with the Jani? How do you know them?"

Kotler huffed and shook his head. "Remember about a year ago, when I went to Denver to give a talk? I ... had a visitor. Someone knocked on my door, and when I opened it, he had a gun on me. He also had about a foot of height and a hundred pounds of muscle on me. The guy was massive."

"You never told me this," Denzel said, his voice stern.

Kotler shook his head. "No. I didn't. And it's because, in the end, that guy wasn't my enemy. Not exactly. His name was Granger ..."

"Granger? Jeez, Kotler, where do these guys get these names?"

"He said it was his call sign. Like Scope," Kotler replied.

"Call sign," Denzel said. "Like maybe ex-military?"

"I think these guys do have military training, but I think it goes deeper than that. The Knights of the Jani are a secret order, kind of like the Templars. In fact, Granger indicated they're an offshoot of the Templars. They've been operating in secret for centuries, gathering artifacts and objects that could have some influence on the world stage. They store them in a vault, in the Temple of Jani."

"And what do they do with them?" Denzel asked.

"Protect them," Kotler said. "From the people who might use them to take control of the world."

"People like Scope?" Denzel asked, dubious.

"People like Hitler," Kotler replied. "During World War II, Hitler was obsessed with retrieving artifacts that he perceived as items of great power. He employed historians and other experts, and sent teams to all points on the globe, with orders to retrieve anything they could find."

"Teams like the Blue Division," Denzel nodded, putting it together. "He sent them here, to find something."

"That's what I think," Kotler agreed. "Something hidden in these caves. Something we definitely do not want Scope and his men to find."

"But I thought you said the Jani were the good guys?" Denzel asked.

"Yes and no," Kotler replied. "Their methods can be a little ... extralegal. But there's another problem. After I was ... *recruited* to help Granger, another Jani came after us with an armed force. His name was Talon. He and his men were a recent offshoot of the Jani. A rogue faction that wants to gain access to the Jani vaults, to use the artifacts and the information stored there to take over the world."

"Take over the world?" Denzel scoffed. "Like a comic book villain?"

"Exactly like a comic book villain," Kotler said, smiling. "Secret lairs, items of great power, men with no scruples. The Bond film writes itself."

"You say items of great power. What does that mean, exactly? Like the Ark of the Covenant, from Indiana Jones?"

Kotler sighed. "I loved those movies. *Kingdom of the Crystal Skull*, though ..." He drifted for a second, then shook his head. "Ok, think of it this way: The deeper we dig into the histories and comparative mythologies of ancient cultures, from all over the world, the more we start to suspect that there were technologies at play that have been lost to us. There are ancient sites where the stone has been carved and placed so perfectly, you can't slip a sheet of paper between them, even thousands of years later. Those same structures tend to be constructed of such immense stones that even modern construction equipment couldn't move them, and yet they were transported from quarry sites hundreds of miles distant and stacked atop each other to great heights.

"All of that is a strong hint, but then we keep uncovering older and older structures, buried deeper within the earth than should be possible, hinting at civilizations that are *epochs* distant from modern day. Think of the Other World site we found in Egypt. I haven't been allowed to study any of the artifacts from that site, but Dr. Maalyck has told me he suspects most of it may be older than the Giza complex."

"Ok, so these things can be really old," Denzel said. "But that doesn't mean magic is real."

"Are you familiar with Arthur C. Clarke?" Kotler asked.

"Of course," Denzel said. "The author. He wrote *2001*."

"Among hundreds of other books," Kotler nodded. "He once said, 'any sufficiently advanced technology is indistinguishable from magic.'" Kotler reached into his pocket and took out his phone, waving it for Denzel to see. "Imagine if I could show this to people living in the first century. A device that can communicate with someone on the other side of the planet, that lets me carry thousands of books, watch videos, listen to music, even see maps of the terrain as if I'm floating high above. Can you imagine what early humans would make of it? How could it be anything other than magic?"

"So you're saying that ancient cultures had technology that was beyond our understanding," Denzel replied.

"Maybe some of them did," Kotler said. "Maybe some of them had technology that could carve tunnels like these," he placed his hand on the smooth wall, "in months or even days rather than years. It's a technology we don't have even now, as advanced as we are. What do you think someone like Hitler would do with technology like that?"

"Got it," Denzel nodded. "So you're worried that the Jani here might be more like the bad guys you encountered in Colorado? The rogue faction?"

"I have no way to know," Kotler said, shaking his head. "So I have to assume the worst."

Denzel nodded. "Ok. I'm with you. But unless we can figure a way out of this that doesn't get us killed, I don't know how we can help with anything."

Kotler was about to reply when a voice called loudly to them from deeper in the tunnel, echoing from the stone walls. "Dr. Kotler. Agent Denzel. I believe I can help."

Kotler and Denzel looked at each other, and Denzel got to his feet, weapon at the ready.

"Who is that?" Kotler called back.

"An old friend," the voice said. "Or, an old ally. It's me, Dr. Kotler. It's Granger."

16

GRANGER LED them back through the tunnel they'd used to escape, taking the lead. To Kotler, Granger looked too big for this environment, his massive and muscled frame filling the tunnel and blocking any view of the path ahead.

He seemed unconcerned over having his back to Denzel, who remained armed and ready, even hyper alert.

Kotler assured Denzel that they were safe. Or safe enough, at least. "Besides," he said, "I'm betting there are a lot of really well-armed men in the amphitheater right now. We don't have much choice but to trust them."

Denzel, of course, would only trust them so far, but he did trust Kotler at least, and he grudgingly went along.

As they walked, Kotler and Granger caught up.

"Things have gotten a little more dangerous since we last met," Granger said. "The rogue faction is better organized than we first thought. After the events at Cheyenne Mountain, we learned that some of the other vaults around the world have been raided. Safe houses were exposed and turned out. A lot of good men have died."

"I'm sorry to hear it," Kotler replied. "How many vaults do the Knights of Jani have around the world?"

Granger chuckled. "Nice try."

"What kind of stuff are they taking, when they get these vaults?" Denzel asked.

"Artifacts and documents, mostly. The really important items are now under guard in the Temple of Jani, within Cheyenne Mountain. We've fortified the vault there. The trouble is, it's challenging to know who among us has joined the New Gods and who hasn't."

Kotler and Denzel both stopped, and seconds later Granger seemed to notice, pausing and turning around himself.

"Did you say 'New Gods?'" Kotler asked.

"You've heard of them?" Granger replied.

"I've encountered them twice now," Kotler responded. "Under two different names. In a village in the Scottish Highlands, they were calling themselves *Diathan Ùra*. More recently, at a dig site in Egypt, they were operating under the name *Alihat Iadida*. Both names mean 'new gods,' in Gaelic and Aramaic, respectively. I suspected they were the same organization, and now it seems I was right."

Granger nodded. "We think the localized names are meant to keep various groups siloed from each other. There's an idea—a criticism of the Jani—that we're too centralized, and therefore too easy to target. The rogue faction wants to break our order into territories, each with its own version of the vault in the Temple of Jani. Each cell empowered to be 'new gods,' to rule their territory rather than hide in the shadows."

"And what about you?" Denzel asked, his tone openly critical. "What do you want?"

Granger looked at the agent, his expression hard and

unwavering. "Me personally? I am loyal to the order that my father and his father and generations of my family have belonged to for centuries. An order that most have never realized was there, influencing the events of history."

"You can see where most folks wouldn't be thrilled to know something like that existed," Denzel replied.

Granger shook his head and sighed. "Most people allow their lives to be determined by whatever random events happen to them. The Knights of Jani choose, and act on that choice, for the betterment of humanity. People think they're afraid of people with great power, but they're really afraid of wielding that power themselves. The Knights of Jani exist to wield power on behalf of those who cannot."

"Sounds like horse crap apologetics," Denzel said.

Granger studied him, then chuckled and nodded. "Yeah. There's a lot of that, too." He turned and led them the rest of the way out of the tunnel, back into the amphitheater where they'd only recently been the captives of Scope and his men. As they emerged, Kotler saw that the place had undergone a transformation since he and Denzel had made their escape.

There were more lights now, for a start. Equipment had been brought in and was being set up on temporary tables. Dozens of men were moving and working, briskly attending to tasks.

"So the helicopters and the ground forces," Kotler said. "That wasn't the police, was it? All you?"

"All us," Granger nodded.

"Where's Scope?" Denzel asked, looking around.

Granger shook his head. "He and two of his men managed to escape. We think they're in one of the tunnels. I have scouts down most of them, but I don't have enough people to search each tunnel all at once. It was sheer luck that I happened to pick the one you used."

"Luck," Kotler said with an ironic tone.

"It happens," Granger shrugged. "Though I admit, I tend to think of it as synchronicity. Or the influence of God."

Kotler nodded. The Knights of Jani had their roots in the same clouded, near-mystic origins as groups such as the Knights Templars and the Teutonic Knights—religious orders with a military tradition. Their name, "Jani," was a Hebrew phrase translating to "gift from God," another name for Christ. But the word "Jani" was also represented by the Georgian symbol of the same name—a symbol resembling a tilted Christian cross with a horizontal line at its top.

The Jani Sigil, as it was called within this order.

Kotler had done some digging since his encounter with Granger and the Knights of Jani, and though there was little to uncover in official historical records, he'd managed to find a few scraps and hints among archived journals and documents. The order had kept itself well-hidden throughout history, but the traces were there. And by all indications, the Jani were a benevolent organization—self-appointed guardians of the most dangerous artifacts and documents that history had produced, to prevent their use by would-be despots and dictators.

Which made the "New Gods" all the more startling and intriguing, as an offshoot of the Jani. In most ways, their goals and designs were in direct opposition to those of the order. The rogue organization was on the hunt for anything that could give it power and influence, so that its members could become gods themselves. Metaphorically, perhaps, but Kotler suspected that many of the organization's members might just believe they could achieve real, super-natural power, and rule mankind by whim.

Whether or not it was possible to harness supernatural forces to respond to their whims, the fact was that there were plenty of dangerous items in the world. Kotler was uncomfortable enough knowing that the Jani were out there, as a self-appointed police force of history. He much preferred that over the alternative, however: That these dangerous resources might become tools in the hands of unchecked and unregulated world leaders, despots in waiting.

So on the whole, in Kotler's estimate, it was better for the Jani to exist and to keep up their mission. But the fact that after all of these centuries an offshoot of the organization had essentially become the very thing the Jani were pledged to fight—that was a frightening prospect.

What could have created such a split in an organization that had managed to survive intact for centuries, adhering to its mission to protect humanity from unmetered, unchecked power?

"You found us pretty quickly," Kotler said, shaking off the trance of his thoughts. "No sign of Scope and the others?"

"Not yet," Granger said. "But Scope and his men are very highly trained at this sort of thing. They know how to keep a low profile."

"Are you guys ex-military?" Denzel asked.

Granger shrugged. "Some of us are. We use whatever resources we have to make each Knight worthy of the title. Our lineage stretches back for hundreds of years. Maybe more. It can be hard to know for sure. We tend to lock away records of the order so that only a chosen few can know our history. But many of our order have served in the military of various governments if only to learn combat skills or to assess their technological capacity. It's a way for us to train without being noticed."

"Hiding in plain sight," Kotler said. "And, I assume, learning the weaknesses of those military operations. Just in case."

Granger looked at him for a moment. "I'd like it very much if you and Agent Denzel would assist us in preventing Scope and his men from finding whatever they're after."

"And help you find it for yourselves, right?" Kotler asked.

"To protect it," Granger nodded.

"How do we know you won't just use it the way Scope intends to?" Denzel asked. "You can see why I might not be comfortable with any of this, seeing as I'm a Federal agent, sworn to uphold US law."

"I would never ask you to do anything that violates your oath," Granger said.

Kotler knew this was deceptive. Granger wouldn't ask, because he would force Denzel and anyone else to do what he believed needed to be done. What Kotler wasn't sure about was how far Granger and his people would go. Would they kill the two of them, if they refused to participate?

"You should know that Scope mentioned reinforcements are coming," Kotler said.

Granger nodded. "We're aware. The New Gods aren't the only people who have double agents."

"There are also police on their way," Kotler said, guarded.

Granger looked at him, then nodded. "You don't want them getting hurt," he said.

"No," Kotler said. "I'd rather no one got hurt."

Granger turned to one of his men, leaning in close to whisper orders that Kotler couldn't hear. The man left the amphitheater, down what Kotler now thought of as the Snake trail—the exit to the outside.

He turned back to Kotler. "My men will take care of the vehicles outside these caves. That should buy us some time. We're setting up equipment to help us locate whatever is here, as quickly as possible. But I believe you could speed that along."

"I'm not sure I could outpace whatever scanners and technology you're bringing into play," Kotler said.

"Don't be so sure," Granger chuckled. "I've come to realize that you have a special knack for intuitive leaps. The sort of thing even our best equipment can't match."

"That's not all he has a knack for," Denzel grumbled. "He's also pretty good at getting us into situations like this one."

"And out again, at least," Kotler said, a bit defensive. He looked at Granger once more, considering, then sighed and shook his head. "Please don't make me regret this."

He took his phone out of his pocket and brought up the photo of the map. He glanced around, found a table with some surface cleared, and took the Spanish papers from his pocket, spreading them flat. He placed the phone on top of these as a weight and a quick reference.

Granger and Denzel joined him, leaning over to see what he was showing them.

"These are the documents that brought us here in the first place," Kotler said. "A good man died because of these. Killed by Scope." He gave Granger a pointed look.

Granger, to his credit, nodded somberly. "I'm sorry that happened."

Kotler let that pass. He pointed to the phone. "The

papers were in a leather portfolio that had this map burned into it, hidden in plain sight. Something I know you can appreciate," he glanced up to see that his joke landed with Granger, who merely nodded. "This is how we found this place. The swastika was the clue."

"Swastika," Granger said. "Nazis."

"The *División Azul*," Kotler said, pointing to the phrase on one of the pages. "The Blue Division. A Spanish arm of the Nazi forces. They fought primarily on the Eastern front, against the Soviets. But I think Hitler recruited some of them to come here, to the United States, in search of something hidden among the native cultures here. You see these sketches?" He pointed to the papers. "There are symbols from the Hohokam, the Maya, the Navajo. Hitler was looking for something among the indigenous groups here."

"That would be in line with his actions throughout World War II," Granger nodded.

Denzel asked, "Did you already know about this? About the Blue Division?"

Granger shook his head. "Not specifically. But we do know that Hitler was sending forces all over the planet, to any sites where he might find items of power. The Jani spent those years constantly moving, making sure the vaults stayed secure and out of Hitler's reach. It was one of the reasons that the Temple of Jani was moved to Colorado. A central repository for some of the more dangerous items."

"This temple," Denzel said, eyeing Granger pointedly. "Is that something the US government should know about?"

"What makes you think they don't already know about it?" Granger smiled.

Denzel grumbled under his breath.

Kotler shook his head and continued. "So the map also contains a series of symbols, and I've been working on what they mean. I think I'm onto something, but it's an incomplete idea. I realized while we were in that tunnel, where you found us, that there is a symbol on the map that matches it, and that each of these map symbols might correspond to one of the tunnels radiating from the amphitheater."

Granger studied the map. "Do you know what this means?"

Kotler shook his head. "No, not yet. I'm working from the theory that it's a distraction. Camouflage, meant to keep anyone from immediately working out where this place is."

"Which you managed to figure out anyway," Granger said, smiling.

Kotler shrugged. "Maybe I got lucky. But I'm also thinking the map gives more detail about this place than might be obvious at first. I haven't had a chance to really look this over since working out that we were actually standing in one of the symbols, but I think we may have everything we need to find what we're looking for."

"Do we actually know what we're looking for?" Denzel asked.

Kotler shook his head but noticed that Granger's body language shifted. He became guarded, his face set and his shoulders tight.

"I don't," Kotler said cautiously, "but it looks like you do."

Granger shot him a look and then sighed. "He's looking for the *Popol Vuh*."

Kotler's eyes widened, and his jaw dropped. "You're kidding!"

"What's a Po-po view?" Denzel asked.

"Popol Vuh," Kotler correctly absently. "It's a K'iche' term, translating to 'book of the community.' It's ... well, it's more or less the equivalent of the Old Testament, among the people of Central America—a written record of the oral tradition of the K'iche' people, in Guatemala. Among other stories, it contains a creation myth, and one with striking similarities to the Judeo-Christian tradition."

He looked at Granger. "But the manuscript is in a museum in Guatemala City. I've seen it. I've even been allowed to hold it and study it."

"It's there," Granger nodded. "But an original copy of it may be here as well. Along with a cache of documents and artifacts that were rescued from the Spanish, during the purge of Mesoamerican mythologies."

"Purge?" Denzel asked.

Kotler shook his head. "When Europeans first came to the Americas, they brought with them a mission to convert the natives to Christianity. Spanish Conquistadors accompanied Dominican priests and friars for this purpose, and for years they slashed and burned any historical and mythological records they encountered. Some of it survived, thanks to a change of heart by some of the priests. Francisco Ximénez was a Dominican priest who helped to preserve the Popol Vuh, writing it down in parallel columns of phonetic K'iche' and Spanish, side-by-side. It's one of the few surviving records of the history of that people."

"So the Spanish just came in and wiped it all out? No thought to preserve it at all?" Denzel shook his head. "Between this and the Nazi thing, I'm not getting a very good impression of the Spanish."

Kotler laughed. "Well, it's not all bad. The Spanish are responsible for a huge swath of things that benefit humanity, including advances in science and technology. Many people credit Johannes Gutenberg for inventing the printing press, but moveable type was actually invented by

Spanish Muslims almost a century earlier. Gutenberg's accomplishment was more about democratizing print, making it accessible to the masses."

Denzel nodded. "Uh-huh. But here and now, there's a copy of this potpourri voom ..."

"Popol Vuh," Kotler interjected.

"... here in these tunnels?"

He and Kotler both looked to Granger, who sighed. "We don't know exactly, but we believe so. We think this may be a vault."

Kotler blinked. "A vault? As in a vault of the Jani?"

"An early one," Granger nodded.

Kotler considered this, his eyes going wide. "Wait," he said. "Are you saying that the Spanish operatives who came here, the members of the Blue Division who were working for Hitler ... were they also Knights of Jani?"

Granger smirked and shrugged. "You have to ask yourself: If Hitler sent them here to retrieve these things, why didn't they end up in Hitler's hands? How did they end up in a system of mountain caves in the Sonoran Desert, rather than carted and shipped back to Nazi Germany?"

Kotler stared for a moment. "Ok," he said slowly. "I think maybe this just got twice as interesting. Let's go see what it was that Hitler wanted."

17

KOTLER, Denzel, and Granger were accompanied by four of Granger's men as they entered the most promising tunnel.

"What makes you so sure this is the one?" Denzel asked.

Kotler shook his head. "It's not that sure of a thing, but going by the papers and the map, I believe it has the best odds." He unrolled the papers, showing both Denzel and Granger under the light of his headlamp. Granger had let them gear up from the supplies brought in by the Jani, and Kotler was thrilled that this included a .45 ACP in a holster hanging at his side. He hoped he wouldn't have to use it, but he felt a lot better being armed for once.

"Look at this symbol," Kotler said, pointing. "Ricky called it a rocket ship, and I think the Spanish operatives may have seen it the same way." He took out his phone then and brought up the photo of the map. "Here," he said, pointing to a swirling ring.

"What does that swirl have to do with a rocket ship?" Denzel asked.

"It's a Hohokam symbol, and one that isn't really translated anywhere. But I think it represents the Milky Way."

"The Milky Way ... galaxy?" Granger asked.

"Out here, in the Sonoran Desert, on a clear night ..." Kotler waved to the stone ceiling above. "You could see forever. With no light pollution, and on a moonless night, the stars would stand out like street lights on a hillside. The Milky Way would certainly be visible to the naked eye. I believe that's what this symbol represents. And if the Spanish believed that too, then they might have used the 'rocket' as a clue to where they hid the vault."

"Like the swastika," Denzel said. "A symbol they knew their people would recognize."

"It may not have had its negative connotations yet," Kotler nodded. "The Blue Division was formed only two years after Germany's first volley into World War II. At that time, the swastika was still just a symbol the Nazis co-opted from another culture. Depending on when the Spanish operatives came to the Americas, they may not have thought of it as a symbol of evil, at the time."

"Fair enough," Denzel said. "But you're saying you think this swirly symbol means 'Milky Way,' and that the rocket ship in the papers means we should go here?"

"Exactly," Kotler nodded, smiling. He rolled the papers and put them back in his pocket. "It's the best clue I have, at the moment."

"It's good enough for me," Granger shrugged.

They kept moving, deeper into the stone tunnel. After a time the path started to turn noticeably to the left, in a wide arc that eventually obscured their view. "Here's where the swirl starts," Kotler said.

"I take it we're going to walk in circles for a while?" Granger asked.

Kotler nodded. "It's going to be a bit monotonous. But I'm about 92% sure we're on the right path."

"Not the certainty I would have preferred," Granger groused.

"This isn't an exact science," Kotler shrugged. "We're working from papers and a map that are nearly a hundred years old, based on symbols conveying concepts from multiple thousands of years ago. An 8% margin for error is pretty good if you ask me."

They walked on for a solid hour, following the curve of the tunnel as it led them deeper into the mountain. Denzel paused for a moment to take a pull from his canteen. "I think we're on a downward gradient," he said, nodding in the direction they were moving.

Kotler took out his own canteen and opened it, pouring a bit of water on the floor. It flowed in a tiny rivulet, moving downhill in the same direction as they were walking. "You're right," he said. "Judging by the amount of slope, if that stays consistent, we'll be pretty deep underground by the time we reach the center of this. That ... doesn't make sense."

"It doesn't?" Denzel asked. "What's wrong with it? Wouldn't whoever built this want to bury the vault as deep as they could?"

Kotler shook his head. "It doesn't mesh with the theory that this is a mockup of a spiral galaxy. The builders would have wanted to go up, not down. They would want the vault to be closer to the sky gods—closer to the real galaxy above."

"You're sure about that?" Granger asked.

Kotler shrugged. "Well, being sure about it doesn't make much difference if reality contradicts me. So I think maybe there's something else at play." He considered, and then looked to the map on his phone. After a moment he made an excited noise. "Of course! I can't believe I didn't see it!"

"See what?" Granger asked. "Something we need to be aware of?"

"In a sense," Kotler said. "Look, see the swirl? It's oriented so that the galaxy is spinning in a counter-clockwise direction. That mimics the swirl of the Milky Way. So from our perspective, these tunnels should be turning to the right."

"But they're turning to the left," Denzel said. "Clockwise."

Kotler nodded. "It's reversed. I can't believe I didn't notice it before. And it's sloping downward. Both of these facts would make sense if ..."

"If this was a mirror image of the real galaxy," Granger said, smiling. "Very clever. But does this change anything for us?"

Kotler shrugged. "I have no idea. But it might be good to keep in mind. In a sense, we are ascending to the heavens right now, even though we're moving downward into the Earth. In that way, the spiral is completing a sphere. The Milky Way above, and these tunnels below."

They started moving again, and Kotler kept thinking about what these new revelations meant, trying to come up with any potential dangers or issues that might flow naturally from the way this place was designed. So far, they had yet to encounter any traps or other hazards in this place. In fact, the entire network of tunnels extending from the amphitheater appeared to be wide open for anyone to explore, once they knew it was there.

That, in itself, was intriguing.

There was a theory in the archaeological community— an idea that at first was eschewed by mainstream archaeologists but was now gaining some traction and popularity. The gist was pretty simple: Maybe some of the ancient structures that survived to modern day, such as the pyramids of Giza, the Sphinx, the Aztec and Mayan temples, the stone heads of Easter Island—maybe these remnants of ancient civilization were actually all part of a network of machines.

Not machines as modern humanity might think of them. No moving parts or circuits, no pressure or conduction, no digital or mechanical output. Instead, these might be machines meant to make people ask questions.

The idea was simple but profound.

Many of the world's ancient sites were built with such precision, and on such an immense scale, that some speculated they were meant to withstand great cataclysms and profound swathes of time, so they would last long enough for some future, advanced civilization to study them. And knowing that any form of written record might be either destroyed, worn away by erosion, or potentially rendered untranslatable due to lingual drift or extinction, the builders relied on the inherent mathematics of the structures themselves, as a vocabulary for the language they transmitted across eons.

Kotler had been enamored of this idea for years. After all, what better way to preserve even just a sliver of a culture's history and science than to build something that would force the observer to ask questions?

Why did these ancient cultures build pyramids or lay immense stones? How did they transport them? How did they cut them with a precision that was greater than what could be accomplished even with computer-guided lasers in the modern era? What was the purpose of it all?

More intriguing, however, was the fact that many of

these structures, from all around the globe, conformed to mathematical principles that were thought of as beyond the ken of ancient cultures.

The Great Pyramid, as an example, was constructed in such a way that the ratio of its base to its height perfectly conformed to a mathematical representation of the northern hemisphere of the Earth—something ancient Egyptians purportedly knew nothing about. And yet, there it was, in the ratios of each side of the pyramid, to its height and width.

The purpose for this remained unclear, but Kotler and others speculated that it might be a message. In effect, it might be ancient Egypt's version of "You are here."

The implications of this, of course, were profound. For a start, if the Great Pyramid represented the Earth, what did the other two pyramids represent? One might be the moon. But what of the other? Mars? Or were there once two moons orbiting the Earth? Or did these two pyramids represent two other planets altogether? Or none at all?

And, of course, there was the fact that all three pyramids were aligned in the same pattern as the three stars in Orion's belt—something that had been hotly debated and disputed but never quite debunked by mainstream science.

Some archaeologists had concluded, then, that the reason the pyramids were built was so future humans would ask questions such as these. The pyramids—indeed hundreds of ancient sites worldwide—were "question machines," constructed to force curious and intelligent minds to speculate and contemplate, and to ultimately draw conclusions that might just lead to the truth.

Kotler believed this was as plausible as any idea he'd ever encountered. He was intrigued by what it meant, if true. Because any machine designed to force people to think and reason and ask questions had to have had an ultimate message to transmit. And so far, modern humanity had not been smart enough to translate that message.

Here, in these precisely carved tunnels under a mountain in the Sonoran Desert, Kotler was starting to get that same vibe. He was beginning to feel a nudge at his subconscious. He was starting to think there was a message to translate here, practically begging for him to stop, to think, to supply an answer.

They had been marching in this spiral for close to two hours before they noticed the curve was getting tighter, the turns coming more frequently. By Kotler's estimate, they were approaching the center of the spiral. It might turn up any minute now.

Granger, Denzel, and the Jani paused long enough to ready themselves for whatever might come next. Kotler, too, made sure his weapon was loaded, a round chambered and waiting, in case it was needed. It was possible that Scope and his two men had come this way—they hadn't yet been found in any of the tunnels that Granger's men had already explored. And though they were outnumbered, they might have the advantage of a fortified position.

As part of their preparations, Granger used his radio, trying to reach his team in the amphitheater. The digital device was more advanced than standard radio technology, which Kotler found intriguing. It operated on a very narrow band and had enough power to send its signal through stone, metal, and most materials. But only to a point. This far down, miles below the amphitheater and with so much rock between them, even this advanced technology wasn't cutting it.

"It'll keep trying to send my signal," Granger said. "It pulses every few minutes, scanning to see if it can connect. We may get an update if we're lucky."

"Alright," Denzel said, standing armed and ready. "Let's go see what this is all about."

They marched on, and after rounding just another couple of tight turns, they emerged into a cavernous space. The tunnel ended at a ledge, and a set of perfectly squared stairs descended into the larger chamber. Beyond that, the room opened up into just about the most unusual space Kotler had ever seen.

High above them, huge stalactites hovered like the upper jaw of an enormous stone beast. But on closer inspection, Kotler decided there was something unnatural about them.

For a start, in the whole of their descent into this chamber, everything had been measured and intentional. The tunnel itself stretched from the amphitheater in precise lines, gently curving and sloping downward, leading them inexorably to this space. And yet, once they arrived, the space itself seemed to emulate a natural cavern. The stone looked rough and natural. The signs of meticulous sculpting were gone. Except ...

"Those aren't stalactites," Kotler whispered.

"Sorry?" Denzel asked.

Kotler looked to the rest of the men, who were all staring dumbfounded at the stone landscape before them. "It's upside down," Kotler replied. "Those aren't stalactites. They were carved into the ceiling of this place. They're a model."

"A model for what?" Granger asked.

Kotler looked at him, his face beaming with fascination.

"For these mountains," Kotler said. He gestured upward. "Someone carved them in the ceiling. Those are the mountains we're standing in, right now." He looked back to the baffled faces of the men standing next to him. "We're looking down on a mountain range."

18

"Detective?"

Kozak turned, cup of coffee in hand. He was stirring in a mound of non-dairy creamer and Splenda with a tiny, plastic stir stick, without much luck. The coffee was currently the consistency of overly watered fresh cement, and it wasn't going to get much better.

The uniform at the door of the breakroom held up a pink phone message. He handed this to Kozak, who read it while sipping from his cup of sludge.

Kozak swallowed and cursed, tossed the Styrofoam cup and its contents in the trash and marched out through the bullpen, to the parking lot. He was in his sedan and speeding away from the station in minutes.

He needed to get to the airfield before the choppers lifted off.

He was just in time, and though there was some protest, he yelled until he had a seat on one of the two birds. Before they had even lifted off, he pulled on a headset and demanded to be connected to the SWAT team leader.

"I'll chew your ass later over why I didn't get any notice

on this," Kozak yelled into the microphone. "You're sure the call came from Dr. Kotler?"

"Affirmative," the officer on the other end replied. "We have four BearCat ATVs approaching over ground. We'll end up beating them there by chopper. Should touch down in about half an hour. Probably two hours for the ATVs, but they're already twenty minutes out."

"How do we know Kotler's not pulling something?" Kozak yelled.

"Sir, we're responding according to protocol. Kotler's message was on the SOS band. He said there was an armed threat. He described a chopper and at least three well-armed men, possibly more at the mountain. We're doing this by the playbook."

"Playbook," Kozak said, his voice dripping with contempt. "When we land, first thing I want is Kotler in handcuffs. If his FBI buddy is with him, I want him cuffed too. We'll hold them until I know what this is."

"Yes, sir."

Kozak settled back then, watching the city of Mesa slide by as they rose and moved toward the desert.

This was Kotler screwing with him, he knew. Rich know-it-all, trying to shift the attention away from himself with a made-up terrorist attack. Kozak wasn't falling for it. He figured Kotler for Ricky Miller's murder, and if there wasn't enough evidence to bring him in just yet maybe this would be enough to hold him for 48 hours. He could make it work.

Kozak was only onboard this bird so he could be the one to put the cuffs on Kotler and Denzel personally. He was going to enjoy it. The agent would have to call his superiors and do some explaining, which sure to be embarrassing. It might even be a career ender, if it turned out he was helping a murderer evade capture.

Everything about this case stank to heaven, and Kozak would be glad to have it over.

He settled back, watched the terrain shift rapidly, and wished he'd thought to grab an antacid.

19

As Kotler and the others made their way down the stone steps, they couldn't help looking up occasionally at the miniature mountain range hanging from above. Now that he knew what it was, Kotler found the whole thing very disorienting.

The disorientation lasted only a moment, however, as they reached the floor of the chamber and he looked down to realize what was at their feet.

"My God," he said, taking off his headlamp and turning the beam so that it fell across the cavern floor.

Thousands of glittering protrusions dotted the landscape in all directions, catching the light and glowing with it.

"What is this?" Denzel asked.

Kotler knelt beside one of the protrusions, prodding it with a finger, looking at it closely.

"Quartz," Kotler said. "Shaped and polished crystal, embedded in the floor." He stood, moving the light over the space in a wide circle. "I think these nodules may cover the entire floor of this place."

"What does it mean?" Granger asked.

Kotler shook his head. Something was nagging at him, but he hadn't quite put it together. There was something about this that felt familiar.

He looked around. The far walls of the cavern curved upward from the floor, like a bowl.

"No," Kotler whispered. "Not a bowl." He turned to Granger and Denzel. "A dome!"

"What?" Granger asked.

"An inverted dome. This," Kotler waved to indicate the expanse of the floor. "This is a representation of the night sky, as seen from those mountains." He pointed to the range hovering above them.

"We are standing on the sky, looking down on the earth," Granger said. "Like the gods." There was a slight smile on the giant man's lips. He shook his head. "Amazing."

"Yeah, very cool," Denzel said. "So how does it help us? How do we find what we're looking for?"

Kotler shook his head. "Not sure yet. But come on, Roland, you don't think this is astonishing?"

"It's a very nice floor," Denzel replied. "The crystals are kind of a tripping hazard."

Kotler rolled his eyes and moved across the inverted sky toward the section of wall furthest from them. "Whoever built all this ... they were incredibly advanced. This is beyond anything I could have expected."

"Do you think the Blue Division built it?" Granger asked.

Kotler shook his head. "It would have taken decades. It's not impossible, but I don't get the impression that these men were here that long. I think this already existed, and they discovered it while looking for whatever it was that Hitler had them searching for. The question is, what else did they find here?"

Denzel stepped up, "What about the poppa yo?"

"Popol Vuh," Kotler said, shaking his head. "I don't know. I'm not sure what I expected us to find here, but this wasn't it. I thought we might find signs of a vault, maybe crates or something. But this?"

Granger gave orders to his men. "Start searching every square inch," he said. "Report anything out of the ordinary."

"I think we left ordinary behind awhile back," Denzel said.

Kotler finally reached the wall he'd been aiming for. He stood and put a hand to the stone, which was as smooth as the stone corridors had been. It arched up from the floor and continued on to the edge of the hanging mountains, high above them. He raised the light. "There's something here," he said.

Granger and Denzel joined him.

There in the wall before them was a web of lines and dots. Kotler inspected them closer to find that they were neither etched into nor painted onto the surface of the wall. "They're an inlay," he marveled. "Thin veins of ... I'm not sure." His light tilted as he leaned in for a closer look, shining on the wall at a slight angle. Now that it wasn't head-on, the veins in the wall seemed to pick up the light, glowing faintly.

"My God," Kotler whispered. "It's inlaid with quartz!" He stood back, shaking his head in amazement. "Someone really put some time into this. Fine threads of quartz, laid out in patterns. And the patterns have some regularity. Symmetry. I can see a few repeated motifs. I ... I think this may be a language."

"Does it say something?" Denzel asked.

"Nothing I could read, if it does," Kotler said. He moved a few steps further back from the wall, looking at it from a distance. "Do me a favor, shine your lights on the wall, at an angle. Catch those veins without shining on them directly. Let me see it from back here."

Granger and Denzel dutifully turned their lights to the wall, lighting as wide a patch as they could from their positions. Denzel knelt so that his light would shine from slightly below. Granger moved his light closer, angling it so that it caught his section of wall from the side.

It took some adjustment and repositioning, but in just a moment the entire section of wall lit up, the light conducted along the veins of quarts to illuminate a webbed pattern that rose upward until it faded.

Kotler could see the fine inlay now as a larger pattern. It spread across the wall like a spiderweb suspended between tree branches. Traces of lines stretched in all directions, their points of overlap forming tiny dots. It was a knotwork of lines that stretched well beyond the range of their lights. It might cover the entirety of the wall, from floor to ceiling—a stunning achievement.

"It's incredible," Kotler said, awed.

"What is it?" Denzel asked.

Kotler shook his head. "I can't say for sure, but I think it's a form of knotwork writing."

"Knotwork writing?" Granger asked, perplexed.

"Similar to a form recently discovered in Inca sites," Kotler said. "The markings resemble Incan *khipus*. Which would make this entire space a giant *Khipumayuq*."

"Ok, now I think you're just making words up," Denzel said.

Kotler smiled. "The khipu were first discovered by our friend Franciso Pizarro, in the 1500s."

"The Conquistador guy who slashed and burned all the Central American history?" Denzel asked.

"The same," Kotler nodded. "And he might have destroyed the khipu as well if he'd known they would eventually be translated. These are large collections of precisely knotted threads, sometimes so large that they can hang like a tapestry to cover an entire wall of a temple. Though, I've never heard of one this immense." He shook his head as if to reset his perception. "Most of what's been translated to date is census information, but it hints at something profound about the Inca. They had a writing system after all. Far different than anything the Europeans had ever encountered. Which may be why it survived to modern day, undetected. It means there could have been a great deal more to their culture than we've ever realized."

"But you cannot read the writing here?" Granger asked.

"I'd need a lot more time to study it," Kotler nodded. "Something for another day."

"Does this relate to our search for the Popol Vuh?" Granger asked.

Kotler shook his head. "I don't believe so. Even if it does, it's a dead end for now. We should keep looking."

There was a chirp from Granger's radio. "Granger, we've found something."

"Signal me," Granger said into the device.

From across the chamber, they saw a red glow waving slowly in the darkness.

They made their way to the spot, where Granger's men were gathered around a section of wall. They were shining lights on a series of staggered nodules of stone protruding from the wall's surface, stretching upward from the floor until they disappeared in the darkness far above.

"Is it me, or do those look like rock wall handholds?" Denzel asked.

Kotler leaned in to inspect them closer. "I think you're right," he said. "Look at the stagger pattern. They're spaced so that someone could use them almost like ladder rungs. The question is, where do they lead?"

In answer, Granger freed his hands, clipping everything he'd been holding to his pack. He adjusted his headlamp, clipping it back to the band around his head, and then grasped one of the nodules, lifting himself upward with such ease that it stunned Kotler for a moment.

In seconds Granger had climbed several feet, high above their heads. He looked down at them. "Join me?"

Kotler sighed. "I really have to get to the gym more," he said, grasping a nodule and lifting himself upward with considerably less ease than Granger had displayed.

"Wait a minute," Denzel said, putting a hand on Kotler's shoulder. "We have no idea what's up there, or how stable those holds are. You're just going to free climb?"

Kotler glanced up. "I figure Granger weighs about a hundred pounds more than I do. If anyone is going to pull one of these handholds loose, it'll be him."

"Not the point," Denzel said.

"Roland, whatever the Blue Division found, they brought it here. We know that much, at least. And we know that the New Gods have people coming. It could end up in a firefight, at which point we won't really have any time left for this search. This isn't ideal, but it's a lead. We're going by gut now. And ... well, I have this feeling."

"What feeling?" Denzel asked.

"This place," Kotler motioned to the darkened expanse all around them. "It's here to tell us something. It's a message. The way it's built, the tunnels and the walls, the quartz stars and inlays, the mountain range—everywhere I look, I see a machine. A machine designed to make me ask questions. And this is just ... part of it."

Denzel studied him for a moment. "You ever done any rock climbing?"

"Quite a bit," Kotler grinned. "Not enough recently to prepare for something like this, but I'll get by."

"Agent Denzel," Granger called down. "If you would not mind, I would prefer if you stayed on the ground with some of my men. The rest can join us up here."

"What for?" Denzel called back.

"Call it a hunch," Granger said. "But I believe we may need you there."

Denzel said nothing, and Kotler lost track of him as he began climbing, struggling to keep up with Granger's fast-paced ascent.

The height was dizzying, and Kotler soon became very conscious of the fact that they were free-climbing a stone surface in a darkened cavern. He stopped for a moment, calming himself with several deep breaths. "I don't suppose anyone brought any actual climbing gear. Ropes? Harness? Pitons?"

One of Granger's men spoke up from below. "If we had such things, wouldn't we already be using them?"

"Fair point," Kotler sighed, and pushed on.

Up and up they went, the darkness pressing in around them. Kotler's arms burned with the effort, and his hands ached. He kept moving, however, and gradually realized that they were climbing at a slight angle, as if this section of wall bulged away from the center of the room. It would do little to keep him from falling to a painful death, should he slip. But the higher they rose, the more the downward press of gravity helped to adhere him to the wall, rather than threaten to pull him from it.

Soon they were climbing onto a near-horizontal surface, a bulb of stone high above the floor of the cavern. Eventually, it was easier to stand and walk than to climb, and Kotler did so with great relief.

Granger was waiting for him, standing with his hands on his hips, looking out over the cavern floor below. As the other two Jani joined them, Kotler edged forward as far as he dared, until he was able to see the headlamps from Denzel and the Jani down on the cavern floor.

As they moved, their lights bounced and reflected at irregular intervals from the nodules of quartz embedded in the floor, giving the impression of a field of twinkling stars.

I've seen something like this before, Kotler realized. *The Other World.*

In a cavern system in Egypt, Kotler and Denzel had encountered another stone chamber created by an ancient civilization. That one had held a trove of artifacts and artwork depicting ancient gods from a broad swathe of pantheons from around the world. It was an incredible find, and one Kotler had desperately wanted to study. But his run-in with the *Alihat Iadida*—the local Egyptian branch of the New Gods—had created a political situation that made his presence at the site untenable to the Egyptian government. At least for the time being.

Perhaps someday he'd be able to return.

For now, looking down at the glittering floor of this space, he was struck by the similarities, and the questions arose again. If this was, in fact, a "question machine," it was certainly doing its job.

Kotler thought about the New Gods. An offshoot of the Knights of Jani, with all the resources and history of that organization. They might just pose a more significant threat than Kotler had imagined.

When this was over, he intended to find out everything he possibly could about the New Gods.

For now, he turned to Granger. "Well, we're up here." He looked out across the cavern, shining his light outward. It caught the carved ridges of the hovering mountains. "This is just mind-boggling."

"It isn't over yet," Granger said.

Kotler looked back to see the man pointing to the wall just a few dozen feet from them. "An opening," Granger said.

Kotler peered, seeing its edges as the Jani moved closer to it, their headlamps catching the precise cuts of stone. He nodded, and he and Granger moved forward. Granger used his radio to alert the crew on the floor as to their status.

Kotler put a hand almost absently on the .45 ACP, touching it lightly just for reassurance. His gut feelings were starting to encompass more than just the questions this place was nudging within him. They'd encountered only minor dangers so far, but he suspected that was about to change.

He continued his march into the darkness.

KOZAK GRIPPED a handrail as the chopper pivoted in the air, settling to the ground in a rapid but smooth bump. It had been a while since he'd been in one of these birds, and even longer since he'd been in a passenger seat. Thirty years on the force and he'd managed to avoid helicopters. Ten years of them in the Marines had been plenty, he'd always reckoned. He'd make an exception this one time.

The second chopper came in behind, landing on a higher point of the ridge after making a circle of the area. Over the headset, Kozak could hear the report—no signs. No vehicles. No terrorists. No Kotler.

As the doors of both choppers opened, the SWAT officers were out and on the ground in seconds. Kozak trailed behind, crouching, letting them do their thing.

Sharpshooters took positions on the rocks overlooking the base of the mountain. Several of the team moved in patterns, sweeping their paths for any signs of danger. There were no lights in use—nearly everyone but Kozak had night vision goggles. The sun had started to fade while they were in the air, and it was nearly dark on this side of the mountains, with just enough light for Kozak to pick things out.

Several minutes went by with nothing happening.

"Well, ain't this something," Kozak said aloud. "Looks like Kotler ..."

"Detective!" One of the men shouted as he jogged forward. He was holding a small, orange device that looked like a walkie-talkie with a tiny keyboard on its face. "This is the GPS unit Dr. Kotler used to signal us."

"Bag it," Kozak said. "It's evidence."

The SWAT team leader walked up. "Evidence? For what?"

"Kotler just pulled a false alarm. I'm adding it to the list of charges. He's in the wind."

The team leader, Captain Estevez, shook his head. "Something doesn't add up here, Detective. What would he gain by a false alarm? It's not like the whole department is out here. You wouldn't even be out here if you hadn't ... *talked* your way onto one of my birds."

Kozak heard him but wasn't sure how to answer him. He fell back on his default management approach, leaning in and scowling. "I got a murder suspect hightailing out into the desert while under investigation and sending an SOS that leads a bunch of cops to a big, fat nothing," he shouted. "You think that might not be just a little suspicious? He's trying to throw me off his trail! Fake terror attacks? Here? What's anybody attacking here? He said there was a Jeep and a helicopter parked out here. You see *any* of that?"

Estevez shook his head and was about to reply when suddenly there was a roar from over the ridge. Everyone turned, taking cover, weapons aimed at a sudden flurry of activity in the air.

Four military-style helicopters banked and encircled

them, and in seconds the SWAT team was surrounded, and in a dangerous position.

Chaos erupted as the firefight started, with door gunners laying into them, cutting through both police choppers with a stream of high-powered rounds. The SWAT officers leapt for any cover they could find, returning fire reflexively. There were screams and shouts for medics as officers took hits.

Kozak dove for cover behind a clump of rocks and brush, unholstering his weapon and taking aim. He hesitated, not wanting to waste a shot. The chopper he had in his sights turned, and gunfire strafed the ridge, pinging from the rocks just in front of Kozak, sending chips of stone flying into his face.

Kozak ignored them and steadied his aim, firing twice.

The gunman in the door of the chopper took a hit, reeling backward, and the mounted gun swept wildly, eventually turning too far and perforating the tail of the aircraft, sending it in a crazy spiral until it crashed into the side of the mountain.

It shouldn't have happened, Kozak knew. There was a pin in place on guns like those. It must have been sheered or, worse, removed—allowing the gun to rotate beyond the safe zone. A once-in-a-lifetime hit.

Kozak smiled at the accomplishment, but then realized he was having trouble standing. His left arm felt numb. *Heart attack? Now?*

He cursed, and looked down, realizing that he was safe from a heart attack after all.

He'd been shot. And it was bad.

Blood poured from his arm, dripping to the sandy ground at his feet. A pool was growing alarmingly fast around his scuffed brown loafers.

Kozak dropped to the ground, taking cover again as the remaining helicopters buzzed and circled. He ripped his tie from around his neck and did his best to cinch it above the shot, trying to staunch the flow of blood. One of the SWAT team dropped in beside him, taking over and tying off the wound. "Sir, we'll get you back ..."

"Back to what, boy?" Kozak interrupted. "Those two birds are down! Just aim and shoot!"

The officer nodded and took position, raising a long rifle. One of the sharpshooters, Kozak realized.

Kozak himself rolled over, feeling lightheaded and aching, the pain in his arm only barely registering with all the adrenaline pumping through him. He raised his weapon again, one-handed, and measured each shot, trying to replicate his luck with the first chopper.

Luck might not be a strategy, but by Kozak's estimate, it was the best they could hope for. They were outnumbered and outgunned. The injuries and deaths were piling up on their side. The bad guys had the advantage of a higher vantage point and more firepower.

Things were not going to go well.

And that was when the miracle happened.

From the foot of the mountains, below their position, spotlights suddenly erupted in piercing beams, sweeping the night sky and targeting two of the remaining helicopters. The third was nowhere in sight, which Kozak took to mean it had landed somewhere, probably putting boots on the ground so they could circle around and take out the bedraggled SWAT team.

"What the hell is happening below the ridge?" Kozak shouted.

"I ... it looks like armed men are coming out of the mountains! They're helping us fight back!"

Armed men? Were the terrorists they came here to arrest actually helping them fight? Kozak shook his head. It was crazy, but he'd take crazy over dead.

"Get on your radio. Tell your people that one of those birds is on the ground. Be ready for a ground assault."

"Yes, sir!" The younger man immediately relayed what Kozak had told him, and then returned to taking shots at the passing helicopters.

Engaged on two fronts now, the birds were playing cautious, rising higher and moving out over the mountains. They'd find a place to land, Kozak knew. They'd put people on the ground and then run air support. They were going to pin the SWAT team and their new allies in, take everyone out from the outside.

"How long before the ATVs get here?" Kozak shouted.

"Half hour!" the officer replied. "They're pushing as hard as they can!"

It wasn't going to be soon enough. This fight would be over by then, and it wasn't a sure thing the good guys would win.

Kozak glanced down the ridgeline, to the blazing ruins of the enemy chopper he'd helped to shoot down. He then looked back to their own birds. They were riddled with bullets, but that didn't mean they were down for the count. He rolled until he could climb to his feet.

"Sir, stay down!"

Kozak cursed the younger man, and moved forward, staggering but keeping upright. His left arm hung useless at his side, and in his right hand, he gripped his service weapon. He stayed low and kept moving. When he got to the helicopter, he pulled open the door, finding the pilot slumped and bloody. Dead.

"Sorry pal," he said, pulling the man free. He was as

gentle and respectful about it as he could manage, but one-handed and injured, he was only just able to ease the man to the ground without flat-out dropping him there.

He shouted to the SWAT shooter, who was still taking shots from cover. "Get over here!"

The younger man took one more shot and ran for Kozak. Once he arrived, Kozak ordered him into the back of the chopper. "We're going to take a page out of their book! Buckle up!"

"You can fly this?" the shooter asked, dubious.

"Took my tour in the 70s and 80s, got almost ten thousand hours behind the yoke. It's been a while, but I can work it if it can still fly."

With no further questions, both men climbed inside, and Kozak ran through a vaguely remembered flight checklist, spinning things up, awkwardly handling the stick as they rose into the air.

Kozak didn't pray all that often, but he was doing it now like he'd been in church every Sunday his whole life.

21

DENZEL WASN'T happy about being relegated to tagging along with the Jani, but he was fine with not making a free-hand climb up a sheer rock face, with nothing but head-lamps to light the way. He'd already had an experience like that, in Antarctica. So he hadn't put up much of a fight when Kotler and Granger started scaling their way upward and wanted him to stay on the ground. He would have done it, and he worried for Kotler, but he trusted that Kotler was capable and knew what he was doing.

Now, however, Denzel wondered what good he was doing here on the ground. He started to eye the grips on the wall, considering whether he should follow.

"Agent Denzel," one of the Jani called to him.

Denzel looked up and then moved toward the three men who were studying another section of the inverted dome, several feet away. They were kneeling, casting light on something on the ground. Denzel peered at it and shook his head, unsure whether he was really seeing what he thought he was seeing.

There on the ground of this vast and ancient structure,

which held secrets that Denzel could only hope to understand by watching a special on the History Channel someday, was a Snickers wrapper.

"They've been here," he said. He looked at the Jani who
had called him over. "What was your call sign?" Denzel
asked.

"Rictor," the man replied.

"Like Richter scale?"

"Like the comic book character," Rictor grinned. "But
yeah, more or less. I'm an expert in explosives and tectonics.
Call signs can be on point sometimes."

"Ok then," Denzel said. "Get on that fancy walkie talkie
and tell Granger that the bad guys are definitely here, and
probably up there with them."

Rictor nodded and relayed the information.

Denzel turned to the others. "They might still be down
here somewhere, so we'd better ..."

"Agent Denzel!" Rictor interrupted. "You need to hear
this!"

Rictor tapped a button, and the radio started playing a
series of cross chatter from someone running an operation.
It was occasionally broken, skipping as if the digital signal
was only barely getting through, but it was pretty clear what
they were hearing. Terse commands and demands for status
reports were punctuated with the unmistakable sounds of
combat.

"This is coming in from a relay—a repeat of earlier chatter. I can't tell how long ago, but it sounds like our people
are engaged in combat outside. And the police have
arrived."

"The police?" Denzel asked. "Your people are attacking
the police?"

"No," Rictor shook his head. "It sounds like the New

Gods are here, and we're assisting the police in fighting them back."

"It doesn't sound like it's going well," Denzel said, his adrenaline spiking. "We need to get out there and join the fight."

Rictor nodded, turning to the others and issuing some commands. He looked back to Denzel. "Granger says they got our message, and that we're approved to head out."

"So glad," Denzel scowled. "Let's move."

They raced back to the stone steps, taking them two at a time until they reached the upper ledge. They had made their way at a steady but careful pace through the spiral, their first time through. It had taken hours. Now that they knew what to expect, Denzel reasoned, they should be able to cut that time at least in half.

The truth was it was a long and winding path, and there could be danger at every turn. Until they could reach an area with a reliable signal, and get updates from the other Jani, there was no way to know whether the enemy might have infiltrated these tunnels. They could be waiting for them.

Denzel and the others were running hot, armed and loaded. Ready. He hoped.

He wasn't sure what good they would do, once they reached the fight. But he couldn't stand by and let good men die without doing something to help.

They ran the tunnel, weapons ready, willing to face whatever unknowns lay ahead.

22

"Acknowledged," Granger said into the radio. He lowered it, clipped it to his vest, and eyed Kotler. "Agent Denzel and my men are going to assist in the firefight up top."

Kotler took this in, nodding. "We should keep searching," he said solemnly. "I think we may be running out of time."

"I agree," Granger said. "But I need you to know—we cannot allow the New Gods to get their hands on any artifacts that might give them the power they seek."

Kotler said nothing. Whatever the cost, the Jani would keep the Popol Vuh and any other artifact out of play, even if it meant destroying them.

Even if it meant dying in the process.

They raced on, all the more cautious now that they knew that Scope and his men were here somewhere. Kotler took the .45 ACP from its holster, ready to use it if it came to that.

These tunnels, high above the inverted dome, were shorter and narrower than those they'd entered through. It was a good thing Denzel had stayed behind, Kotler mused. His claustrophobia was likely already a tingle in his gut, a tension in his neck and shoulders. A space like this one would put a lot more pressure on him. It was even giving Kotler a touch of anxiety, though that could be attributed as much to the threats they all faced as to the uncomfortable proportions and dimensions of these tunnels.

He glanced at Granger, who was forced to stoop and hunch as he walked or risk banging or scraping his head on the low ceiling. Despite this, the man moved with studied grace, his every step measured. It hinted at Granger's training, which made Kotler all the more curious about him—about all the Knights of Jani.

The tunnel took a turn ahead of them, veering to the left. When they rounded the corner, the floor rose sharply upward, at an angle steep enough that it caused some strain and effort. Kotler found himself breathing heavier, his legs and lungs burning from the effort. Another bend to the left and the floor leveled out again.

"What was that about?" Kotler huffed as they continued to press forward.

"I think we are now above the ceiling of the main chamber, moving back toward it," Granger replied.

"So we're entering the hanging mountains," Kotler nodded. "I figured there would be some significance there. No one would go to the trouble of building a replica like that without some purpose in mind."

They were moving at a rapid pace now—fast enough that Kotler was sweating and huffing from the exertion. He was gratified to see that Granger and the two Jani Knights were experiencing the same. Kotler had started to think of them as superhuman, and it was good to know he was at least close to being in their kind of shape.

The corridor stretched on until suddenly the light from their headlamps revealed an opening ahead.

"Be ready," Granger said.

Everyone double-checked their weapons and vests, and there was a muffled clatter of rounds being chambered and straps being tightened.

As they reached the opening, they slowed, pressing against the walls on either side of the corridor and peering into the space beyond, sweeping with both lights and weapons.

As Kotler inspected the room before them, his heart raced.

"The vault," he said quietly.

The room was large, though not as cavernous as the inverted dome below. It was also brimming with treasures— everywhere Kotler looked there were stone tables and shelves, row after row of them, and each covered with arti- facts that hinted at their considerable age and historical significance. Not every item within Kotler's range of vision was Native American in origin. This was a storehouse of world history. A vault of the Jani, just as they had anticipated.

Intrigued and enthralled, Kotler stepped forward, agog with wonder, only to be jerked suddenly backward by Granger.

"Careful!" he shouted.

Kotler felt a jolt, and shook himself, bringing himself back to where he was. He had been so focused on the vault that he hadn't fully taken in his surroundings.

Kotler looked down to the floor and felt himself go cold.

At his feet, just a step away, was a void that stretched from wall to wall across the floor of the room.

Kotler shined his light down into it, brightening the

beam to its fullest. In the distant depths, far below them, he caught the faint glimmer of stars, reflecting back his light.

"The inverted dome," Kotler said, his voice quiet, filled with awe. "We're in the hanging mountains, high above the floor."

"You were nearly back where we started," Granger said, his voice stern. "Be more careful."

Kotler made a wry face and nodded sheepishly. He'd gotten too caught up in the excitement of discovery and had become too complacent after the lack of traps and other security measures, up to this point. If this place really was built as a question machine, as a test of the intelligence and readiness of the discoverer, it made sense that it might save the biggest and perhaps the most fatal questions for the end.

Intelligence belied complacency.

He passed his light over the room beyond the void, illuminating rows of shelves and artifacts, and then turned back to the wide gap in the floor. "That has to be about ten feet," he said. "There's no way we could jump that."

"There must be another way," Granger agreed. He turned to his men. "Split up and search. Be very cautious."

The men went in separate directions, moving along the edge of the drop, looking for anything that might get them across.

Kotler, too, was searching.

There was something about the arrangement of this room, after the long and twisting path that led them here. It tickled at his subconscious, hinting that he should know this. Or that he should at least be able to figure it out. There, across the void from them, was a tantalizing trove of treasures. The knowledge and wisdom of dozens of ancient cultures might reside there—the equivalent of the library of

Alexandria for the Americas, perhaps. All one had to do was bridge ten feet of open air.

Open air that led to the stars, Kotler thought.

"Down is up," Kotler said aloud.

"Excuse me?" Granger asked.

Kotler looked at him. "Since entering the spiral tunnel, everything about this place has been inverted. The spiral galaxy, turning clockwise instead of counterclockwise. The inverted dome representing a starry sky. The replica of the mountains hanging from the ceiling. Everything about this place, from the amphitheater to this gap in the floor, is about making us ask questions. Making us think."

Granger considered this. "What question can we ask that would allow us to cross this void?"

Kotler thought about this and replied. "The first question that comes to mind is, why is everything upside down here?"

Granger frowned. "Do you have an answer?"

Kotler looked around, then nodded. "We should be looking up. Which is to say, we should be looking *down*."

He stepped closer to the gap in the floor and turned his light once again to point toward the distant field of stars below. It was a pretty clean drop. Not the way back down that Kotler would prefer.

As Kotler moved, however, his light occasionally caught the edges of the peaks of the hanging mountain. He was just about to inspect this closer when Granger's men returned.

"I've found something," one of them said.

They followed him to a spot at one end of the room, where the wall curved to continue on past the void, into the room beyond. The Jani used his light to shine across to the opposite side, where there was a jumble of what looked like aluminum rods and rope.

"Rope ladder," Granger said. "They were here."

"How'd they get it anchored over there?" Kotler asked.

Granger's man responded, moving the beam of his flashlight. "They lassoed that thing. Some kind of protrusion from the floor."

Kotler squinted to see it in the faint light. "Looks like maybe a statue or something. Possibly a stone totem." He looked to Granger. "Do we have one of those ladders?"

Granger shook his head. "Unfortunately we do not. We have no rope, either."

"That seems like an inconvenient oversight for people exploring a system of mountain tunnels," Kotler frowned.

Granger shrugged. "We have plenty of rope in the helicopters. I admit it's something we should have brought. But we did not."

"So it is what it is," Kotler said, shaking his head.

He was holding the headlamp in his hand like a flashlight, having forgotten to clip it back in place after his sweep of the void moments earlier. On a whim, he moved the beam along the curved wall of the room, and then downward, through the gap in the floor.

They were near one of the outer peaks of the hanging mountains, and the beam of light brought out the craggy details perfectly. Again Kotler marveled at the level of effort and technology it had taken to create this place. The details were incredible.

He stopped moving; his light fixed on one spot below.

"What is it?" Granger asked, turning to peer down alongside Kotler.

Kotler moved closer to the edge, widened the beam of the light, and smiled. "I think I just found our way over to the other side." He looked up at them, grinning. "Are you ready for a leap of faith?"

23

KOZAK GOT BACK into the groove of flying as if he'd never retired from it. Even one-handed, it was a piece of cake. This bird was far more modern than the last one he'd flown, with all sorts of bells and whistles, assistive technology that made getting back at the stick like getting back on a bicycle.

They moved in a wide circle at first, banking slightly and then leveling out so that junior—the SWAT sharpshooter Kozak hadn't yet learned the name of—could take his shots.

Exactly as Kozak had predicted, the bad guys had boots on the ground. Armed men were circling and swarming, getting ready to put the hurt on the SWAT team on the ridge, and taking positions to pick off the men who had come pouring out of the mountain.

Junior started taking aim, and *ping-ping-ping* the bad guys were going down.

"You buckled in?" Kozak shouted into the radio. "Because we got incoming."

He spotted one of the three remaining helicopters

buzzing toward them from over the mountains, a spotlight glaring into them, trying to blind them.

"I'm stable!" Junior shouted back.

"I'm turning to give you a shot!" Kozak bellowed, shoving the stick to one side and leveling them, turning in air as smoothly as a ballet dancer.

He couldn't see Junior and couldn't even hear the shot over the noise of their own helicopter. But he saw the effect.

The enemy bird seemed to lurch suddenly and then veered off at an angle that was far too steep for safety.

A dead-man's pitch, Kozak thought. *Junior got the pilot.*

"Whoo-hoo!" Junior shouted.

"Don't get cocky, kid," Kozak replied, though he was pretty impressed himself. "We got two more birds out there somewhere."

"Did you just *Star Wars* reference me?"

Kozak chuckled and turned them into a dive, moving them closer to the ground so Junior could start taking shots at some of the snipers gathering on the opposite ridge.

It was working, but it had a drawback. Being this close, and stabilizing the chopper to be a shooting platform, meant making them an easier target for the bad guys.

A series of pings hit the metal of the chopper, and one chipped through the glass in front of Kozak. He cursed and pulled back, turning and rising, presenting a better-armored section of the bird while making them a moving target.

"You good, kid?" Kozak yelled.

"I'm hit!" Junior replied. "Took a hit to my leg. Hurts like hell!"

"You going to live?"

"I'll live!"

"You can keep shooting?"

"Already taking aim!"

Kozak laughed loud and hard at that, surprising even himself. He turned them one more time and buzzed the bad guys who were trying to sneak up on the SWAT team. He held the stick with his knees and made a quick flick with his good hand, hitting a switch on the panel, engaging the bullhorn mounted to the nose of the chopper.

"SWAT Team! Got rats swarming to your South! Enemy on your Southern flank!"

He leveled the chopper then and positioned them so Junior could do his work. As he watched, two bad guys went down. Then, as if his warning had been a rallying call, several SWAT members rushed forward, guns blazing, overwhelming the enemy by sheer speed and grit.

"Good boys," Kozak said, and only then realizing the bullhorn was still active. With his arm injured and his other hand working the controls, he couldn't reach over to flick the switch and turn the bullhorn off.

He laughed. "Screw it," he said, his voice booming over the battlefield below. "Let's take 'em down, boys!"

He turned the chopper again and felt his heart thump as he saw the two enemy helicopters bearing down on him. They both turned, and the gunmen in their doors became plainly visible.

Kozak cursed and gripped the stick with his good hand.

"Hang on Junior!" he shouted, and his voice echoed through the mountains.

24

Denzel and the two Jani finally reached the length of tunnel that was outside of the spiral—the straight path that would lead them directly back to the amphitheater. They were already hearing the sounds of combat up ahead, echoing from the stone walls, funneling to them like a dreadful preview of what was to come. Each man was armed and ready, protective vests in place and weapons raised. They moved forward, alert.

Dozens of people were in the amphitheater when they arrived. The place had been turned into a makeshift triage, and wounded were being treated on the tables, on the floor, anywhere there was room. Among the injured, Denzel saw the occasional SWAT insignia. Police officers, turned allies in this fight by their mere presence, were getting the same care as the Knights themselves. That told Denzel plenty for the moment.

He and his two companions rushed to the entrance tunnel, joining a small contingent of Jani who had been patched up and were returning to the battlefield.

After making their way quickly through the long,

snaking tunnel, Denzel emerged into the night air for the first time since he and Kotler had been abducted. The scene out here was quite different than it had been earlier.

Helicopters buzzed in the night sky, spotlights swept the ground, and door gunners pumped rounds through mounted guns. Smoke and dust rose in clouds that flashed with muzzle fire and glowed from spotlights. The noise was deafening, between chopper engines and gunfire, and it encompassed Denzel like an ocean wave as he stepped out into the fray.

And the voice.

Denzel heard laughter echo from the mountains, and a voice like a grizzled, modern-day god from above, bellowed, "Hang on Junior!"

It took a moment to realize the sound came from a police helicopter that was taking fire from two of the enemy choppers.

Denzel watched as the police chopper spun and wobbled, taking hundreds of rounds from the two enemy birds before finally angling toward the ground, trailing a plume of fire and black smoke before crashing just to the other side of the ridge.

"We need to get to that chopper!" Denzel yelled.

His two companions nodded and followed; guns raised. They all moved in crouching runs between stone outcroppings, staying tight to the rising ridge as much as possible.

They were spotted by the enemy at one point and ducked as automatic fire danced in a trail, nearly catching them before they managed to take cover among the stones. They returned fire, Denzel covering Rictor and the other Jani as they broke for a more secure spot. They returned the favor as Denzel raced forward, keeping the enemy pinned down long enough for the agent to make it to them.

Another contingent of Jani started firing on the enemy then, engaging them as Denzel and his men moved on, pressing toward the fallen helicopter just around a bend in the ridge.

There was enough light coming from the fight that it was reflecting from the haze of smoke and dust, casting a form of diffused faux twilight on everything. It gave Denzel and team a way to see what was ahead of them, but also made their moves visible to the enemy.

They had to chance it. If there was anyone left alive in that fallen bird, they would need medical attention.

Denzel and the others pressed on, and finally, the wreckage of the helicopter became visible.

Scanning the hills around them, Denzel decided it was worth the risk to sprint across the gap between the ravine wall and the wreckage. He signaled the others, and they moved, covering each other in short bursts until all three of them were kneeling near the hulk of crumpled metal. They holstered their weapons and started sifting through the wreckage, calling for anyone who might be alive.

"Here!" a voice said. Denzel and the others pulled away a hunk of metal to reveal a young SWAT officer. He was severely injured and looked to have taken a shot to the leg. One of the Jani used a knife to cut the harness straps that held the man in place. They pulled him free, taking a moment to liberate the man's rifle as well. One of the Jani slung this over his shoulder.

"He's in the front," the SWAT officer said, his voice low and raspy.

Denzel nodded and started pulling away debris, looking for the pilot.

It was a real effort. The chopper had gone down more or less nose first, and there was glass and twisted metal everywhere. But as they worked at it, they were finally able to open a gap.

Denzel gasped, standing back briefly and shaking his head in disbelief.

"Detective Kozak?"

Kozak was in lousy shape, unconscious and bleeding from a head wound. There also seemed to be a lot of blood coming from his arm.

Denzel shouted for help, and together the three able-bodied men pulled away more of the wreckage until finally the Detective could be pulled free.

The two Jani got to work on building a stretcher for Kozak, and Denzel knelt beside the SWAT officer. "Can you walk?"

The young man nodded. "I think so. Going to ... hurt like hell."

"We're going to try to get you to the caves. There's a triage in there. They can treat you."

The man made an attempt to stand, and then cried out, collapsing to the ground. "I ... I can't," he said. "Shot in the leg. It's useless."

Denzel nodded. He turned back to the Jani, looking to Rictor. "You two get Kozak back for medical attention. I'm staying here."

They agreed without argument. They'd completed the stretcher, built from harness straps and metal debris, and now gingerly loaded Kozak aboard. They started making their way back, pausing just long enough to use one of their radios to ask for cover and assistance on their route and to get some help for Denzel and the SWAT officer. "Take this," Rictor, handing over his radio.

Denzel took it with a nod, clipping it inside his vest. He

watched the Jani as they jogged away, with Kozak strapped to the makeshift stretcher between them.

He looked down to the SWAT officer, and then rummaged through the wreck of the chopper until he found a First Aid kit. It wasn't much, but he was able to pour some alcohol on the wound and wrap the leg in gauze. The bullet was still in there, but Denzel had no way to remove it.

"You have your sidearm?" Denzel asked.

The man patted his hip.

"Keep it ready," Denzel said. He stood then, peering around the wreckage, surveying as much of the battlefield as he could from this angle. They were pretty well out of the soup in this spot, at least, but that could change at any moment. For now, Denzel decided their best bet was to stay put and stay alert, and hope that the Jani pulled it out and won this fight.

He hoped they won this fight.

He wasn't at all sure how he was going to get out of this one.

25

Kotler and the others stood at the edge of the precipice, the void opening below them with a sheer drop to the distant floor. Along the wall, molded into the carved shape of the hanging mountains, Kotler could see the ledge. It was just barely visible in the beam of a flashlight, obscured by a slight overhang that would have been the rise of a ridge if these were the actual mountains.

It was a target small enough and far enough out that it was going to be a challenge to reach. And missing it meant a plummet to his death. Not his first choice.

"You're certain about this?" Granger asked. "How do you know there will be a way up from that ledge if you reach it?"

"*When* I reach it," Kotler said. "We don't have room for any negative talk." He looked up at Granger, who wasn't sharing his jovial enthusiasm. "We don't know," Kotler said. "It's a risk, but I think it will pay off."

"If you're wrong, you're going to be trapped there," Granger said. "At least until we can come back with some means of reaching you. Of course, you can always choose the express route down."

"I'll keep it in mind," Kotler smiled grimly. "We know time may be against us. I believe this is the way. Everything about this place is hinting that we should be looking up by looking down. The heavens are at our feet. The mountains rise below us. I believe the idea was to ascend—the way across this void is to go 'up.' And up is down."

"I follow," Granger nodded. "Are you ready?"

"Not even a little," Kotler said, then shook himself, rolled his neck, and looked to the Jani who was spotting for him.

The Jani turned two lights, so they aimed directly at the ledge below—a barely-visible hairline that Kotler hoped went deeper into the stone than it appeared from this angle. The only thing giving him any assurance about it was that it was a ridge that would technically be *under* the mountain. Unlike everything else about this carved structure, that line was oriented to actual-up, rather than oriented toward the symbolic up indicated by the starry heavens below. That had to mean it was intended for someone's use. It had to be a clue, left by the builders.

Of course, it could also have been a design flaw. Or a stress fracture. Or just sloppy work. He could be entrusting his life to a sculpting error.

Kotler took a deep breath, counted down from three, and leapt.

Sailing out across the void, he realized too late that he'd overshot. Instead of landing on the ledge, he smacked into the stone and found himself sliding downward.

Sliding might have been too generous a description, however. In truth, he was falling, and scraping desperately along the carved stone, looking for any hand or foothold and trying not to careen outward to his doom.

The ledge was there, though. And Kotler shifted so that he could land on it.

His feet slapped the rock surface, and he threw his body weight forward, rolling onto his knees and putting his hands on the floor to stabilize himself.

He stayed motionless for a few seconds, on his hands and knees, daring to hope he'd made it, allowing the realization to sink in.

He'd done it. He'd survived!

Now ... where was he?

He stood carefully and turned to look at the space where he'd found himself. He moved away from the edge and discovered that he was in a tunnel entrance. One that sloped upward and bent away from the ledge and the outer wall.

This was it.

He went back to the ledge. "I'm alive!" His voice echoed out into the chamber.

"Good," Granger called back. "But are you trapped?"

"No," Kotler said, grinning. "It's exactly what I thought it would be. The ledge opens up into a tunnel, and that goes upward from here. This is here by design."

Granger turned away and spoke with his men. Kotler couldn't hear them, and so he busied himself with setting up his light on the floor, opening the beam so that it illuminated the tunnel entrance and, he hoped, made the ledge easier to see from above.

"We are going to make the leap in intervals," Granger called. "Stand away from the edge."

"Got it," Kotler replied.

He stepped back, pressing against the opening of the tunnel, watching the ledge.

A moment later, one of the two Jani landed on it with a

thwack, crouching and maintaining his balance. He stood then, turning to call back to the men above. "I've made it, moving away!"

He joined Kotler at the tunnel entrance.

The second man made the leap, landing and rolling forward in an acrobatic move, ending up in a crouch. He called back for Granger and moved to stand with Kotler and the other Jani.

Kotler held his breath.

Granger appeared with a mighty thud, and Kotler saw right away that the larger man was having trouble keeping his balance. He was too close to the edge.

Kotler and the other Jani raced forward just as Granger toppled backward.

They managed to snag his arms, but his feet were out from under him, and he dropped like a fishing weight straight down, his boots scraping wildly against the stone.

He was heavy, and his momentum nearly yanked him from their grasp.

The three of them held fast, and with Granger pulling and using his legs for leverage they were able to bring him upward until he lay on his belly, breathing heavy.

"I would prefer not to do that again," Granger said.

Kotler couldn't help himself. He laughed, loud and sharp, and it echoed from the walls of the great chamber below them.

26

THEY MADE their way up the sloped walkway, with Kotler in the lead. It was prudent, now that they'd encountered their first trap, for him to scan their path as they went.

But it did make for slow going.

Kotler swept every inch of the path before them, looking for triggers in the floor or anything else that might set off some unseen danger. After nearly half an hour of this, though, he straightened. "This is taking too long," he said.

"I agree," Granger replied.

Kotler looked at him for a moment, then back to the walls of the tunnel.

Once again, they were in a space that was carved and crafted, by a means Kotler had yet to determine, and nearly perfect in its precision. Like the spiral tunnel that had led them to this place, it was tall and wide enough for everyone to move comfortably.

Inviting us to walk comfortably, Kotler thought.

The tunnel they'd taken after climbing the wall had been narrow and short—uncomfortable both physically and psychologically. Was that intentional? Was there a message built into the design of that corridor? Warning them of danger, perhaps?

"It's still a question machine," Kotler marveled. He turned to Granger and the others. "We had to pass through a set of dangers to get here."

"I'll say," one of the Jani replied. "That jump ..."

"Not just the jump," Kotler interrupted. "The climb, which was designed to be done freestyle. The gap in the floor, a sudden drop at the end of a long and cramped tunnel. The leap of faith to a hidden ledge. From the moment we found that climbing wall, we were challenged. Everything was dangerous. But here, we can stand upright, walk without worry."

"So you're saying this is a message from the builders," Granger replied.

"I believe so," Kotler nodded. "And I believe it means we can move freely."

"You're sure?" Granger asked.

"You keep asking me that," Kotler frowned.

"Because I'm hoping that at least once you'll say that you are."

"I'm not a hundred percent. But let's say maybe ninety-five percent."

"Five percent margin for error," the other Jani said, shrugging. "We've definitely faced worse odds."

"Anything to move this along," Granger said. "I'm willing to risk it."

With that, they started moving at a much faster pace, heedless of any traps that might be hidden here. Kotler had decided that the meta-message from the builders was "Congratulations, you've made it. Welcome."

He might be wrong. But he didn't think so. He had always trusted his intuition, and right now that intuition was telling him that the very structure surrounding them was speaking to them, telling them they were safe. From the intention of the builders, at least.

Maybe he was getting the hang of this—reading notes written in stone and geometry and layout, laid by hands from countless eons ago. It had worked so far, and the more time he spent in this place, the surer he became of his hypothesis—that this was, indeed, a question machine. The builders had intended this place to be a message to the future.

This place ...

Kotler knew this place was impossible. By every standard of mainstream archaeology and science, it was simply impossible. The perfectly smooth walls and straight lines, the symmetry and balance, the advanced architecture and design ...

Impossible.

And yet, here it was.

Kotler considered all of the impossible and implausible things he'd now seen in just three years. Marvels that were legendary in their status. Signs of advanced knowledge, thinking, and science, from cultures that were thought to have been so primitive they hadn't even invented the wheel. Here was just more evidence, more proof, that some advanced civilization had to have existed before the modern age. Someone had to have come before, to have prepared the way, to have tried desperately to communicate with a future advanced generation and leave some part of their story behind.

But why?

What cataclysm had struck, in the far reaches of unrecorded history, that could have wiped such a civilization from the Earth?

Kotler knew better than anyone that even the most permanent-seeming structures could be reduced to granules of sand, given the right event.

He thought about the destruction of ancient artifacts in Iraq and Egypt, during times of conflict. The desecration of statues and artwork in Rome, as the Pope ordered any sign of the ancient Roman and Greek gods destroyed. The atrocity of the Spanish conquistadors raiding Central American history, tearing down ancient temples to reuse their stones as the foundations of cathedrals and churches, and burning and destroying anything that hinted at an origin for humanity that was not in line with the Judeo-Christian story.

Even the most permanent-feeling history had a way of vanishing overnight.

Most recently, there was the fire in Notre Dame Cathedral, in Paris. It was a heartbreaking event that captured the attention of millions worldwide, spread like a viral marketing campaign on social media. Those millions watched in helpless horror as flames and smoke erupted from the roof of one of the most iconic cathedrals in Europe.

Much of the artwork and artifacts in the Cathedral had been saved. Some were damaged and destroyed. But on the whole, it all could have been much worse. The Cathedral—now a charred and smoldering ruin—could be restored, but it had come perilously close to being wiped from the Earth, remembered only in impermanent photos and films. A story of what used to be, with nothing substantial to back it up.

Nothing lasts forever.

Except, perhaps, things that were *designed* to last forever. Structures built with the sole intention of lasting, of continuing on through countless eons, of being forgotten by history only to be rediscovered. A structure like the Great

Pyramids, the Sphinx, Stonehenge or the heads of Easter Island. Or like these very tunnels, carved with laser precision through the stone of a mountain in the Sonoran Desert.

We may never know who built this place, Kotler decided. But the fact that it existed was a message and a legacy unto itself.

It was thrilling to be here, walking these corridors. Kotler was excited about what might turn up. He knew they were on their way to a trove of ancient artifacts—presumably placed here by the Knights of Jani who were hidden among Hitler's Blue Division. The fact that this place had been co-opted by the Jani as one of their vaults made it no less exciting. In some respects, it amped up the thrill even more.

They'd been walking for several minutes when the tunnel opened up before them, revealing a vast room filled with objects and artifacts.

The vault.

Now, on this side of the void, Kotler could see that this place wound and stretched in a meandering pattern throughout the hanging mountains, divided by the inverted valley areas of the carved structure that combined with the shelves and artifacts to form a cluttered maze. It would be easy to get lost in here, spending days or weeks exploring every corner. From just this spot, Kotler could already see objects of intense interest—artifacts from the far reaches of the planet, sharing shelf space with Mesoamerican art and statuary, an incongruous menagerie that nearly had him salivating.

"Be alert," Granger said quietly. "The New Gods are here somewhere."

Kotler had not forgotten. He rechecked his weapon and allowed the Jani to move into the vault ahead of him.

They stepped quietly, moving with precision and caution as they scanned the room for any signs of the enemy.

Kotler began a mental catalog of the artifacts they passed. He was looking for documents—either something on paper or parchment, which he would expect of the Popol Vuh, or something carved in stone or pressed into clay. There were indeed tablets and other forms of writing among the artifacts they passed. But he suspected that what they were after—what the New Gods were after—was a dedicated collection of ancient documents kept in some central location within the vault.

The New Gods sought any ancient source of power, particularly if it came from long-forgotten knowledge. The Popol Vuh didn't necessarily qualify, since it was primarily a creation myth, and was already well documented. But Kotler suspected he knew why the New Gods were looking for it, here of all places.

If this vault contained a copy of the Popol Vuh, perhaps it also contained a trove of lost documents and histories as well. If they found the Popol Vuh here, in this vault filled with ancient wonders, it was likely they'd find other documents that might fit their agenda. The odds favored it.

And, if nothing else, they would have a collection of prized documents and artifacts that would fetch an unbelievable amount of money on the black market—enough to fund operations for decades, by Kotler's estimate.

They heard a sound from ahead of them, and froze, waiting. Each of them stepped back, taking cover and extinguishing their lights. They were suddenly encompassed by pure and complete darkness, listening intently.

With no actual light to stimulate them, Kotler's eyes began showing him flashes and ghosts of light, drifting blotches of color that moved as his eyes moved. It took a moment for his pupils to adjust, but when they did, he began to detect a faint trace of actual light from up ahead.

The New Gods.

They could hear them now, talking amongst themselves. There were only three of them, but Kotler knew that numbers could be deceiving when it came to men trained to be Knights of Jani. Each of these men was highly skilled and capable. And well-armed, Kotler knew.

He heard a familiar voice then—Scope, asking questions and giving orders. Kotler couldn't make out what the New Gods were saying, as their voices were refracted and echoing from the stone of the walls and the artifacts lacing the room. Kotler thought he was catching a word or two here and there, but not enough to decipher any meaning.

He edged closer to Granger. "Any plans?"

Granger signaled his men to come closer, and the four of them huddled behind a towering stone statue, whispering. Granger laid out the strategy he had in mind and each man's role in it. When he was done, he handed Kotler one of the digital radios and gave him a quick crash course on its use. "Put this in your ear," he said, taking a small bud from a small compartment in the back of the radio. "It works on bone conduction, so you can sub-vocalize and still send a message. I've turned off multi-frequency monitoring, so you won't suddenly hear a pre-recorded packet from outside. Just in case a signal accidentally gets through."

Kotler took the radio and clipped it inside his vest, then shoved the earbud into his left ear. Granger's mouth moved, but he made no sound. In his ear, however, he heard an artificial voice say, "We will be able to keep in contact without speaking aloud."

Kotler arched his eyebrows, impressed. "Roger that," he mouthed silently.

"Careful what you say," the robot voice came again, this time from one of Granger's men. "Everything gets recorded in a buffer, when these things are on auto transmit."

Kotler nodded, and then he and the others dispersed, each moving to his own position.

They would leverage the element of surprise, take the New Gods from all sides.

The part that made Kotler uncomfortable was Granger's nonchalant order made all the more chilling as it arrived via the flat, unemotional voice of the radio: "If they do not surrender, kill them."

At this point, Kotler wasn't sure what options they might have, when it came to stopping Scope and his men. But he wasn't fully onboard with wholesale assassination. He had to think of another way.

And he'd better think of it quick.

Granger gave the signal, and the four of them moved.

27

"WE'RE GOING to have to move," Denzel said. "I found a piece of conduit you can use as a crutch." He held it up, one end wrapped in part of a seat cushion, secured with the rest of the surgical tape from the First Aid kit. "I'm sorry, it's going to hurt."

The SWAT officer nodded.

His name was Cole Harrison, and he'd been a police officer for just under five years, trained to be a sniper for SWAT when he wasn't performing his regular duties with Mesa PD. Denzel had pressed him for details about his life as they waited, trying to keep him alert. He'd lost a lot of blood, and though it had slowed Denzel could see that the bandage around Cole's leg was darkening.

They couldn't stay here. Cole needed medical attention, but they were also in the hot zone for this fight. Any minute, Denzel expected one of the enemy to round the wall of the ravine and open fire. They had some protection here, between the rocks and the wreckage, but they wouldn't last long.

Their chances were better if they were moving.

Denzel helped Cole to his feet, and to his credit, the younger officer winced but didn't cry out. He was toughing it out, Denzel knew. It was possible he had more injuries from the crash than were evident from the outside, and they'd both kept silent about this possibility. But Denzel was determined to get him back to the amphitheater for medical treatment if he could.

The problem was, the Jani and the police were currently losing this fight with the New Gods.

Denzel worried about the possibility that he and Cole would be swarmed by New God operatives, who seemed limitless in number. They also seemed to be everywhere, pushing in from all sides, emboldened by their air support.

The damned helicopters.

Denzel pulled Cole's left arm across his shoulders, and the younger man leaned heavily on both Denzel and the makeshift crutch, keeping his right leg elevated from the ground as much as possible. In this pose, they hobbled along, slowly limping away from the wreckage of the police chopper, back into the ravine through which Denzel had arrived.

The trouble with this plan was that they were walking straight back into the fray, with the enemy all around them.

Once they were away from the helicopter, Denzel found a spot where the two of them could hide out for a moment. It wasn't perfect—a craggy hole in the wall of the ravine that allowed them to take cover from most directions but left them visible to anyone approaching from their North. It would do, though, for the few seconds Denzel needed.

He unclipped the radio.

"This is Agent Denzel. I have an injured man, and I'm just West of the Amphitheater. I got a lot of bad guys between me and there. Any chance of some cover? We're coming in slow."

He waited, and a moment later a voice returned over the air. "Agent Denzel, we can't get to your position. We've got a line of enemy pushing against us on the West. You're going to have to find another way in."

Denzel cursed, leaning his head against the rock of the ravine wall. He huffed. "Roger that."

He clipped the radio back inside his vest and looked at Cole, who was leaning on the crutch.

"We can't go back the way we came," Denzel said. "There's no way out of the ravine at that point. We'd be trapped. That means we have to push forward."

"To the amphitheater," Cole nodded.

"Through the enemy line," Denzel said, somberly.

Cole considered this, then pulled his sidearm, checking the chamber.

Denzel nodded and did the same.

They resumed their ambling, stilted walk, limping along a step at a time, eyes alert for any danger nearby.

The pace was slow and painful, and Denzel's anxiety was on the rise.

It wasn't the combat. He'd been in worse, and in worse condition.

It was the ravine.

The smoke, the darkness, the sounds of weapons fire all around them—it all combined with the walls of stone rising to either side of him to make him feel like he was on the verge of being buried. Memories of being trapped in a spider hole in Afghanistan began to surface. His breathing became quick and shallow, his heart rate went up. He could feel the pressure building in his head, the sick twisting in his chest and his guts.

He took a deep, purposeful breath. He pictured wide open spaces. He remembered the meditation Kotler had given him.

I am at peace. I am safe. I am in a wide-open space. I can move freely. I can breathe freely.

It wasn't immediate, but slowly he felt the tension start to ease, the anxiety begin to fade. It stayed just below the surface, but he could handle that. He could deal with it. *Embrace the suck. Feel the fear, take action anyway.*

They were making good progress but were suddenly halted in their tracks when two of the New Gods appeared on the far side of the ridge, above them.

Denzel and Cole started taking fire, and it was all Denzel could do to get both of them to cover, practically dragging Cole across the desert floor. They rolled to the ground, a few small boulders their only defense.

With the first break in enemy fire, Denzel lifted up and started taking shots with his sidearm. The enemy took notice, ducking and returning fire as they could.

Cole squirmed and crawled, getting himself to a better position, and then raised his weapon, taking a steady aim.

He fired once, twice, three times.

The gunfire from on top of the ridge suddenly stopped.

"Hot damn!" Denzel yelled, reaching out and patting the young officer with a solid slap to his good leg. "You are one hell of a shot!"

"Missed with the second round," Cole frowned.

Denzel laughed and helped Cole get back to his feet. They started their trek again, and now any anxiety Denzel felt faded completely, succumbing to the surge of adrenaline and their victory over their would-be assassins.

They were both in good spirits, both moving at a better

pace. Cole was moving with more strength than Denzel had seen from him so far, emboldened by their victory.

The feeling was short lived.

As they rounded the corner of the ravine, they saw before them the tragedy of battle—the bodies lay everywhere, some dressed in SWAT uniforms and others in the more generic black fatigues of the Jani and the New Gods. Telling those men apart was more than Denzel could manage at the moment, but he feared that most of the dead were the good guys.

Someone yelled from across the way, and Denzel and Cole found themselves in the sights of dozens of armed men. They were ordered to drop their weapons.

"We're not going to do that, are we?" Cole asked.

Denzel considered the enemy, the overwhelming firepower, the inevitable fate that awaited them. They stood no chance. They couldn't run, and fighting would only bring on a quicker death.

"No, sir, we are not," Denzel said grimly.

"Thank you for helping me, Agent Denzel," Cole said.

"It was my honor," Denzel said.

He helped Cole to stand using the crutch and then planted his own feet, squaring off with the enemy. Both men had their weapons down by their sides, their grips firm, their knuckles white.

They were ready. If this was it, they were ready.

They raised their weapons in unison, as if on cue.

Before either could fire, however, there was a roar of engines from the other side of the armed men facing them, followed by a sudden cacophony of police sirens and bullhorns, the voices of men issuing orders to drop arms, to stand down, to surrender.

Four BearCat ATVs erupted from the darkened horizon, clawing at the desert soil with all-terrain tires, kicking up even more dust and debris. It was like watching demons erupt from the Earth, full of fury and bitter with rage.

It had a profound effect.

The New Gods turned on the new enemy, firing rounds that pinged from the armored skins of the vehicles. Officers leapt from the ATVs, returning fire, and taking strategic positions. They brought out the big guns—literally. Denzel spotted several Barrett .50 calibers among the officers.

These were men fresh for the fight and outraged by the injuries and deaths suffered by their comrades in arms. They exploded upon the enemy, who were haggard from battle and only just registering the shock of the turning tide. They had, by their own estimate, already won this fight. Now the fight started anew.

The incoming SWAT team quickly overwhelmed the New Gods on the ground, taking out any who were returning fire and subduing others, rounding them up in cuffs and moving them out of play.

The helicopters buzzed onto the scene, but after only a couple of passes, they must have sensed what Denzel was sensing.

The tide of this battle had just turned. The good guys were winning.

One of the choppers made a pass so that its door gunner could lay down suppressive fire, in an attempt to give the troops on the ground a chance to push back. The SWAT officers manning the .50 caliber rifles turned their attention on the bird, peppering it with multiple rounds, striking critical systems. The chopper went down in a plume of oily black smoke.

The remaining chopper banked and increased speed

and altitude. It took its hits but shrugged them off as it made a dead run for the horizon, disappearing into the night.

Denzel and Cole had made their way to cover while the tide of battle turned, and now watched in stunned silence as the impossible unfolded before them.

They'd been prepared to die fighting. Now the fight was over.

28

KOTLER EASED INTO POSITION, moving stealthily among the artifacts and keeping low. The three men ahead of them had set up a couple of portable lights on stands—light-weight equipment they could easily have carried on their backs. Unlike Kotler and his companions, these guys had come prepared for this environment.

It made him wonder what other contingencies they'd prepared for.

It had to mean something, that despite the arrival of Granger and the Jani, Scope and these two New God foot soldiers had come straight here. Scope had tasked Kotler with finding this very vault, but when chaos broke out, he and his men had chosen the right tunnel seemingly at random.

Or was it random after all?

Kotler and Denzel had sprinted down the closest passage to them when the fighting started, and they left Scope unconscious on the floor. But before the arrival of the Jani, Kotler had been working out the symbolism that was the key to this place, mulling over the iconography etched into the columns at the head of each of the thirteen entrances, and considering them in light of what little he already knew.

Realization hit Kotler all at once.

While puzzling it over, examining the network of tunnel entrances, he had reached out to touch those symbols, which surely brought them to Scope's attention. Before that, as Kotler had studied the Spanish papers, he had said something aloud: "Rocket ship."

Kotler silently cursed himself.

Scope was no fool. He was here, in this network of tunnels, precisely because he had some inside information about a copy of the Popol Vuh and the existence of this vault. He had used Kotler to find this place, but he'd also known exactly what this place was, all along.

Now Kotler realized that Scope had been paying far more attention than he'd seemed. He must have heard Kotler's comment and seen the attention Kotler was giving to the groupings of symbols on each column. Scope had put it together, supplemented by whatever additional knowledge he had about this place. Kotler had inadvertently helped him figure this out, at the last minute.

"Sound off," the robot voice said in Kotler's ear, startling him momentarily.

"In position," the voice said. "In position," it repeated.

It took only an instant for Kotler to realize that this was Granger and the two other Jani, subvocalizing to say they were ready. "In position," Kotler mouthed, his voice barely a breath.

"Engage the enemy," the voice said.

The next few seconds were a rush as Granger and the other Jani yelled for Scope and his men to get down, to get on the floor, to keep their hands away from their weapons.

Kotler heard their voices over the earbud, without the robotic inflection, as well as echoing from the stone walls and ceiling.

The three New Gods were taken by surprise, but to their credit, the sudden presence of an enemy was taken in stride. They each leapt to cover, and in seconds they were firing on Granger and the others. Each of them carried P90s —compact, semi-automatic weapons that were perfect for close fighting in an environment such as this.

They had, it seemed to Kotler, been prepared for the eventuality of being discovered.

Granger and his men had better positions, and they were making it difficult for Scope and his men to stay out of the line of fire long enough to make a decent push back. They returned fire, but it was in shorter intervals. Fewer rounds, wider gaps.

Something was wrong.

Kotler had stayed in the position he was given, just as planned, but from his vantage point, he could only see one of Scope's men periodically rising to fire on the Jani. By Kotler's reckoning, he should be able to see all three of them from this position, at least when they rose up partially.

Kotler looked at the space where Scope and the others had been gathered before the attack. It was a room filled with small chests and crates—most of which appeared to be 1940s-era. A sure sign that this was indeed a Jani vault, or at least used as one, and that the Blue Division operatives who had come here had truly been double-agents, turning on Hitler and hiding materials from him in a place where he'd never find them.

That meant that there had been Jani here, sixty years earlier. Here, in this place, having navigated all of the tests and dangers, and finding a way to cross that void.

Kotler realized instantly what this meant, and he turned away from the battle, moving at speed to the outer wall of the chamber where Scope and his men had their lights set up.

"Granger!" Kotler called. "They have a back way out of that chamber!"

There was a pause. "Roger that. Do you have them?"

Kotler realized then that he was the only one in a position that wasn't in danger of direct fire. Granger and the others had inadvertently put themselves in a position where they could only retreat backward, and only at risk of taking a hit from enemy fire. Their "burn the boats" strategy had been to press forward to victory or die trying. It was an effective tactic, but at the moment it was working against them.

"In pursuit," Kotler replied.

He dodged among the statues and artifacts of the vault, darkness growing thicker around him as he moved away from the lights. He kept low, kept his eyes moving, alert for any sign of someone ahead.

Finally, he saw the two men moving among the artifacts. They had a single headlamp going, dimmed so low that it was barely providing any light, but shining like a signal fire to Kotler.

They were carrying something between them—a large crate.

"Get down now!" Kotler shouted, taking aim. "On the floor, hands behind your heads!"

With no hesitation, the two men dropped the crate to the floor and dove for cover. They were firing before they'd even hit the floor. Kotler ducked, but in the first gap in fire, he rose and took aim at the man with the headlamp, taking his shot.

There was a muffled grunt, and the light wobbled widely until it settled, aiming upward to the ceiling, unmoving.

More shots were fired, and Kotler ducked behind a carved stone, moving on his hands and knees to change his position and hopefully get eyes on the shooter.

The light from the headlamp wasn't enough to give Kotler any detail, but it was just enough to silhouette the shooter. When the man turned his face slightly, Kotler was able to make out his features.

"Scope!" Kotler called to him. "You've got nowhere to go! Put your weapon down and surrender."

"Surrender," Scope said, his tone wry and ironic. "Dr. Kotler, you said you'd worked with the Jani before. Do we seem like the type to surrender?"

"But you aren't Jani, are you?" Kotler said. "*Alihat Iadida. Diathan Ùra.* New Gods."

"We do have many names," Scope laughed. "But yes, Dr. Kotler. You've got it. New Gods. That is precisely what we are."

"Even the gods fell," Kotler said.

Scope laughed again. "Yes, that's true. But not this time. When we rise, we will have the power of both ancient knowledge and modern technology. We will have power beyond anything humanity has known for thousands of years, and the might of weapons and resources that have never been seen on the Earth. We are inevitable and unstoppable, Dr. Kotler."

"I'm stopping you right now," Kotler said. Keep your hands up, lie down face down on the floor and ..."

"I'm afraid not," Scope said, and in a motion so quick Kotler barely saw it, the man trained his P90 on the spot where Kotler was hiding, firing round after round, keeping Kotler pinned to the floor.

This wasn't good. Kotler was outgunned and in a bad position. He needed to find a way to turn this around.

He backed away from where he'd been taking cover, and got to his hands and knees again, moving quickly in the opposite direction. He came to a spot where he could see the light from Scope's fallen man, the beam angled upward and casting the room in a weak twilight. Kotler huffed a few times, readying himself, and then sprinted across to that spot.

He could still hear Scope taking a few shots from his position, just feet away. But now Kotler was behind enemy lines. He moved forward.

The New God he'd shot lay on his back, blood pooling around him. Kotler's shot had struck him on the collarbone and had done enough damage to nick the carotid artery. Judging from the injury, the man had bled out soon after hitting the floor. Kotler felt a sick twist in his gut—his earlier hope that he could find a way to end this without killing anyone suddenly faded to a distant dot on the horizon.

This was inevitable.

Things went quiet. Scope was still several feet away, barely visible in the light from the headlamp. Kotler stayed still, watching.

"Have I won, Dr. Kotler?" Scope asked into the darkness. "Have you been hit? I want you to know, if you're still alive, that I regret having to kill you. I think you would have made a fine addition to the New Gods. I had considered making you an offer after all of this concluded. A chance to explore the world's most deeply guarded secrets—the history of humanity that has remained hidden for two thousand years. Possibly more, if some of the Jani legends can be believed. I thought you might be intrigued by that, Dr. Kotler. It's a shame you will now never get the opportunity."

Kotler stood then, stepping forward and pointing his weapon at Scope, who was now crouched behind the crate that he and the other man had been carrying. "Drop your weapon," Kotler said.

Scope froze, not even looking up. Even in the dim light, Kotler could read the man's body language. He'd been caught by surprise, but he was already tensing, preparing to turn, to take a shot and a risk, in the hope that he'd survive, that he'd be victorious.

"Don't," Kotler said.

Scope ignored him, springing like a cat, turning in mid-air and leveling his P90 on Kotler.

Two shots rang into the darkness, joining the sound of weapons fire from Granger and the Jani, facing off against the entrenched New God back at the vault.

The two shots echoed within the chamber, fading from their sharp loudness to a distant echo.

Kotler stood still, feeling himself out, trying to sense the wound.

Scope had missed.

Kotler hadn't.

Scope lay on his back, his weapon falling to the side. Kotler's shot had struck him in the left shoulder and had diverted Scope's shot at the last instant. Now Scope struggled to reach the weapon with his right hand, and Kotler immediately stepped forward, weapon trained on the New God's chest. He put a foot on Scope's wounded shoulder, pressing.

The man screamed, and lay back, his right hand to his side.

Kotler was breathing heavy. He kicked Scope's P90

away and then knelt, gun still aimed, ready. Kotler patted him down, removing a couple of boot knives and other objects that might cause trouble. "Roll over," Kotler commanded.

Scope did as he was told and put his right hand on the back of his head for good measure. His left arm lay useless at his side.

"I would never have joined you," Kotler said. "You should know that."

"They all say that, at the start," Scope said, his voice and breathing revealing the strain of his injury. "Eventually, all serve the New Gods."

"Keep telling yourself that," Kotler said. "Granger, I assume you've heard all of this?"

"Every word," Granger said. We will dispatch the remaining New God shortly."

"Roger that," Kotler said.

He stood for a moment, studying Scope, and shook his head. "What I don't get, Scope, is why you had to kill Ricky Miller. You had to know I had those papers with me. You called in that report to the police, knowing they'd distract me long enough for you to get into my room and take them."

Scope chuckled, though it ended with a slight groan. "We needed you to be motivated," he said. "The man who called you—what does it matter, that I killed him? He was inconsequential. He added nothing to the world. No one will even miss him, now that he's gone. The New Gods have bigger concerns than the life of one old man. And you could still be a part of that."

"Ricky Miller will be remembered," Kotler said, his jaw tight. "You, though ... I'm going to make sure you're put in a hole somewhere and never heard from again."

"Will you have your FBI friend arrest me?" Scope

laughed. "Let me ask you, Dr. Kotler ... do you believe that the Jani have no presence in the FBI? Do you honestly believe that after all these centuries of infiltrating and influencing governments and organizations of power, that we would have neglected to place people into key roles in US law enforcement?"

Kotler said nothing. His grip tightened on his weapon. His finger felt as if it were on the verge of squeezing, of doing the one thing he simultaneously wanted to do but abhorred as a notion. He was an instant away from deciding to kill this man in cold blood as he lay face-down, unarmed.

He relaxed his grip, took a deep breath, and shook his head.

"We have taken the final operative," Granger's voice said over the radio, and Kotler realized that the gunfire had stopped moments earlier.

In his head, he was still hearing it, as if the battle waged on.

29

Denzel waved off the medic, annoyed at the constant prodding. He was fine. He wanted to check in on everyone else.

Cole Harrison, the young SWAT gunner, was sitting with his back against a boulder. His leg had been tended to, the bullet removed, and fresh bandages wound in place. The leg of his pants had been cut off, and he seemed self-conscious about his bare skin showing. He had insisted on keeping the strip of bloodied pant leg and now had it draped to cover himself, at least partially.

Denzel knelt beside him. "Well, you survived," he said. "Good work."

"You, too," Cole smiled. "And thank you. I don't know if I'd have made it without you."

"Oh, no, you'd have died for sure," Denzel said, grinning. "But so would I. We make a pretty good team."

Cole nodded. "Do you know anything about detective Kozak?" he asked, concern plain on his face.

Denzel shook his head. "I'm going to the amphitheater next."

"When you see him," Cole said, "tell him thank you for me. I've never seen anyone do what he did. He was ... just amazing."

Denzel clasped Cole's shoulder and then stood, moving to the entrance tunnel and winding his way to the amphitheater.

His opinion of Detective Kozak had changed a great deal in the past couple of hours. He had thought of the man as a hardass, maybe even a corrupt cop, bent on railroading Kotler into a murder charge. And for all Denzel knew, he might still be hung up on that, even after all of this. Murder charges didn't just go away.

But now he saw a different side of Kozak. The man was a hero, willing to risk everything. He could easily have ducked and kept cover until the fighting was over. Instead, he charged in, heedless of his own injuries, and did what he could to turn the tide of battle.

His actions, Denzel knew, might have been the actual pivot point for all of this. If not for Kozak, they might have lost this fight.

The amphitheater was in a more organized state than it had been when Denzel passed through previously. This was where the most critical patients were being treated. A makeshift surgical theater had been set up, with tarps to help keep dust and contaminants from floating in, and high-powered lamps set up as surgical lights. Denzel wondered if Kozak was in there, being operated on. But as he turned to survey the space, he saw a couple of Jani medics move away from a table against the amphitheater wall, and he spotted Kozak, lying prone on the table.

Denzel moved forward but stopped in his tracks.

Kozak was conscious, and he was propped up slightly, leaning against a roll of material serving as a backrest. He was talking to one of the Jani, who was adjusting an IV drip hanging from a makeshift pole.

He looked uncomfortable and irritable, which seemed reasonable for Kozak anyway. But what had given Denzel pause was the bandages.

The man's right arm had been amputated, the stump wrapped and resting against his side.

Denzel approached cautiously.

"Detective Kozak," he said, his voice low, respectful.

Kozak turned his head slowly and looked at him, his face a mask of annoyance. "Agent Denzel. What's happening out there right now? I heard the cavalry arrived. Do we got any numbers on how many of my people are down?"

Denzel shook his head. "No, they're still figuring things out. The first priority was to disarm and subdue the New Gods."

"The what?" Kozak scowled.

"The bad guys," Denzel said. He took a deep breath and let it out in a huff. "How are you doing?"

Kozak made a face and shook his head. He held up the stump of his right arm. "How do you think? I'm alive, and I'm hoping a whole lot of those bastards aren't."

Denzel smiled lightly. "A whole lot aren't," he said. "We beat them. Thanks to you."

Kozak scowled. "Thanks to a lot of good men and women who fought back hard," he said. "They won't let me get up off this table." He waved to the IV drip. "Lost a lot of blood, and they don't have any. Saline drip is the best they could do."

"I'd listen to them," Denzel said. "Help is on the way. More police, medivacs, even the military."

"How long?" Kozak asked.

Denzel shook his head. "I'm not sure. I don't imagine more than half an hour for the helicopters. They're going to airlift all the wounded out first."

Kozak made a derisive noise. "I've had enough of helicopters to last me the rest of my life," he grumbled.

Denzel smiled. "Just one more," he said. "Then you can be done with them."

Kozak nodded at this and seemed to drift for a moment, his strength waning. He was probably groggy, and Denzel thought he should leave him to sleep.

Before he could move away, though, Kozak asked, "Where's that smarmy partner of yours? Kotler?"

"Dealing with his own thing," Denzel said. He wasn't sure what Kotler was actually up to, at that moment, but it was next on his list, to check into it.

"He's still my suspect," Kozak said.

"You don't figure all of this might change things a little?" Denzel waved a hand to their surroundings.

"There's a whole other can of worms to open up with this bunch," Kozak said, eyeing one of the nearby Jani. "But I got a case to close."

Denzel was about to say something when there was a noise from the far side of the amphitheater.

Two men were being pushed forward by Granger and his Jani subordinates, as they emerged from the opening that led to the spiral tunnel. Denzel recognized one of the men immediately.

Scope.

Behind them, as if he was just out for a casual stroll, Kotler emerged from the tunnel. He was holding a P90 against his shoulder, and he had an air of victory that made him look for all the world like he'd just returned from conquering the enemies of Rome.

He spotted Denzel and made his way forward as a handful of Jani moved to escort Scope and the other New God to the holding area.

"You survived," Denzel said as Kotler stepped up.

"So did you," Kotler nodded, smiling.

"We were just talking about you," Denzel said, nodding to Detective Kozak.

"I still got you figured for the murder of Ricky Miller," Kozak said, though his voice was a bit slurred. Denzel thought there must be more than saline in that IV drip. Probably something to help Kozak calm down and sleep.

Kotler eyed Kozak's missing arm and exchanged a quick glance with Denzel.

He must have read something in Denzel's features. When he responded, it was gentle but also firm. He pointed to Scope, who was being escorted to holding. "That man goes by the handle 'Scope.'" Kotler reached into his vest and took out one of the digital radios the Jani used. "The memory card in this device has an audio recording of him confessing to the murder of Ricky Miller."

Kotler held it up, and Kozak studied him for a moment, then held out his hand.

Kotler placed the radio in Kozak's hand and then showed him how to play back the recording. They stood, listening to Scope's confession. When it was done, Kotler took back the radio, opened its back casing, and removed a tiny memory card. "You can plug this into any card reader and play back the audio file. At the very least, it should clear me as a suspect."

"It's a start," Kozak said, his voice low and muffled. "Don't ... leave town."

With that, the detective drifted into sleep.

Kotler reached into the man's pocket and took out a

bifold wallet. Opening it, he revealed the Detective's badge. Kotler wedged the memory card into the plastic window that contained Kozak's identification. Seemingly for good measure, Kotler took out his phone, lay the badge open on Kozak's chest, and took a photo. He then closed the wallet and put it back in the Detective's pocket, turning and stepping away.

Denzel stepped to join him.

"Aren't you worried that might get lost?" He glanced back at Kozak and shook his head. "Accidentally or otherwise?"

Kotler grinned. "Granger showed me how to edit the clip down, to isolate that segment from the rest of the radio chatter. He also gave me the chip from his radio, so I'd have a copy."

Denzel nodded. "So that's something we can check off our worry list," he said.

Kotler took a deep breath and exhaled in a noisy burst. "One down," he replied.

The two of them walked out of the amphitheater then, intent on getting more details about the approaching support from police and military. The Jani were already moving at a hustle, packing up, preparing for evacuation.

Denzel suspected that by the time backup arrived, this whole place might be a ghost town.

For now, he was ok with that.

He was just happy not to be one of the ghosts.

EPILOGUE

KOTLER AND LIZ relaxed at an outside table, sipping from fresh cups of coffee brought by a waitress who was going out of her way to make up for spilling water into Kotler's lap.

He really hadn't minded. It was something to smile and laugh over, and it had helped to break the slight tension that had hung over the two of them since he'd arrived at Liz's apartment. Laughing over Kotler's wet pants had finally started the conversation they most needed to have.

That same conversation was still going, which Kotler took as a good sign.

He glanced around at the strings of warm, glowing lights scaling like vines along the branches of trees, bridging the gap between the trees and the awning of the restaurant in an inverted arc. The site reminded him of the inverted sky and the hanging mountains, now locked away by military order in mountains of the Sonoran Desert.

There was nothing he could do about that right now.

It was a pleasant night, and the sounds of Manhattan surrounded them. The subtler sounds, from the Manhattan Kotler often missed when he was traveling. The quieter

Manhattan, filled with the wonder of so much to do, so many things to try, so many people to meet, so many corners of this city to explore.

"You're smiling," Liz said, eyeing him over the rim of her coffee cup.

He turned to her. "So are you. I take that to mean we've come to a good place?"

"It means I believe you when you say you want to change your approach," Liz said. "And it means I'm with you, if it's true."

"Was there a chance you weren't going to be with me?" Kotler asked, his eyebrows arched. He was still smiling, though it was tighter, more guarded. Even he wasn't sure if he was ready for the truth. But facing truth was his habit, and he wasn't going to flinch away from it now.

Liz watched his face, and Kotler sensed that she wasn't hesitating because she didn't know how to answer, but was instead weighing what she knew, judging whether it was true or not before committing to her answer. "Yes," she said. "But only a slight one."

Kotler nodded. "I can live with that. I know I've been distant. And I know I fall back on some old habits at times. Bad habits. I'll change."

"I believe you," Liz said, then smiled. "Should we walk?"

Kotler checked his pants. "Looks like things have dried," he smiled.

Liz laughed, and the two of them stood. Kotler helped her with her coat, and they walked arm-in-arm out of the restaurant's outdoor seating, on into the park beyond.

The night was chilled but comfortable, and as they walked the scene opened up like a storybook all around them. A horse and carriage clomped by, a couple seated in back, snuggled together and enjoying the fairytale version of New York. Kotler and Liz were enjoying that fairytale at the moment as well, walking close to each other as if they were just like every other couple strolling through.

They knew the truth, though: They were never going to be like other couples. It was one of the topics that had come up in their conversation. It was something they'd decided to embrace.

"So how did you keep yourself busy, while I was gone?" Kotler asked.

Liz puffed her cheeks. "I have a little side project with Dani," she said.

Kotler frowned. "Dani ... Brown? *Agent* Brown?"

Liz smiled. "That's her."

"Since when are you two the side-project sort of friends?"

"Dan Kotler, you really have not been paying attention to me," Liz said, her expression stern. "I told you she and I have been spending time together."

Kotler chuckled and shook his head. "I'm sorry. From the way you talked about it, I just assumed it was work. So you two are friends now?"

Liz nodded. "Good friends, I think. She's a good person."

"Not my biggest fan," Kotler said. "I think I rub her the wrong way."

"Isn't that how all your friendships start?" Liz asked.

Kotler laughed lightly. "Right," he said. "Roland didn't think much of me either, when we first met. I think I must rub everyone the wrong way."

"Only at first," Liz said, squeezing his arm. "You make up for it."

"Did I rub you the wrong way, when we first met?"

"I was more of a fangirl when we first met," Liz replied, smiling. "So, no. You only started getting on my nerves later."

"Ha, ha," Kotler said in mock injury.

She squeezed his arm tighter, leaning in on his shoulder as they walked.

"Well, I think I'm ready to shake off some of what's been on my mind for the past couple of years," Kotler said, a bit cautiously.

"I think I know what you mean," Liz replied.

Kotler was grateful. Liz was being incredibly generous and understanding, considering what a heel he'd been lately. But while he and Denzel had been in Arizona, Kotler had come to a few decisions about himself and his life, and about his relationship with Liz in particular. Decisions ... and realizations.

He'd been holding Liz at a distance.

She was brilliant, beautiful, and kind. She understood him, he felt. She was a remarkable woman.

Just like Gail McCarthy had been.

Just like Evelyn Horelica, before her.

Kotler's track record with serious relationships hadn't been stellar and had often led to pain and misery on a grand scale. He was objective enough, self-evaluating enough, to recognize that he was letting those experiences color his view of Liz, and of their relationship. He was holding back. And he'd finally realized that holding back with Liz was going to cost him.

So he'd made a decision. He was going to trust again. He was going to explore this, to see where it would lead. He was going to put in the effort.

All of that had hinged on Liz wanting to do the same. But regardless, as Kotler had followed Granger and the Jani out of that vault, climbing back to the floor of the sky chamber and looping their way through the galaxy spiral of the tunnel, Kotler had determined he was going to be all in. If Liz had decided it was over, he would respect that. But he wouldn't assume it, and he wouldn't allow himself to be the roadblock to their relationship any longer.

They walked through the park, and when they emerged at the street, Kotler called for a car. They embraced and chatted quietly, sweetly, until the car pulled up to the curb.

When they arrived at Liz's place, he had the car stand by and walked her up. They kissed goodnight at her door.

"See you tomorrow night?" Kotler asked.

"If I'm not busy," Liz replied, then smiled.

They were still taking things slow—but the pace was more about respect for the relationship than caution on Kotler's part. He was fine with it. Tonight had been a significant leap forward for the two of them.

As he was dropped off in front of his own apartment, Kotler smiled, thanked the driver, and tipped him more than twice the fare. It was a "spread the cheer" kind of night.

He stepped into the lobby of his building and was immediately greeted by Ernest, the doorman.

"Dr. Kotler," Ernest said, waving for him.

Kotler paused as Ernest approached.

"You're still on duty?" Kotler asked. "Kind of a long shift for you, isn't it?"

Ernest smiled. "The night doorman wanted to take his wife to a show. I volunteered."

Kotler smiled and nodded. He often admired Ernest for his attitude—he seemed to genuinely enjoy his work and his role. That couldn't be said for even half the population of the planet, by Kotler's estimate. But as a doorman, and as virtually the lord of the inner workings of Kotler's building, Ernest was a paragon of respectability and genuine joy. He was someone Kotler greatly admired.

Ernest handed him a slip of paper.

"What's this?" Kotler asked, opening it.

"Someone dropped by asking about you, and he said to give that to you when you arrived. He was a big fella. He said you'd understand the message."

Kotler read the handwritten note.

I'll be at Poppa's until midnight. I hope you enjoyed your evening.

"Thanks, Ernest," Kotler said. He smiled and nodded at the doorman, who was studying him, obviously hoping Kotler would explain the mystery of the note. "Just a friend of mine. Playing a little game. Like old times."

"Ah," Ernest said, nodding. "Old college buddy then? Must have been a quarterback!"

Kotler laughed as he took out his phone and arranged for another car. "Something like that," he said.

A few minutes later Kotler stepped out onto the sidewalk and into the back seat of his ride. A few minutes later, and several blocks away, he stepped out of the car in front of Hemingway's.

It was one of Kotler's favorite watering holes—an old-school bar with what may have been the world's most extensive collection of Hemingway-related paraphernalia outside of the Florida Keys. There were photos, signed manuscript pages, even an old typewriter that had belonged to the author himself.

Ernest Hemingway. Or, as some called him, *Poppa* Hemingway. That had been the hint in the note. And judging by Ernest's description of the man who left it, Kotler suspected he knew who he was here to meet.

Kotler was greeted by the bartender, who knew him well. "Hennessy?"

"Black," Kotler smiled.

He scanned the bar, and his eyes fell on a back table, occupied by a massive bulk of a man that Kotler would recognize anywhere by this point.

He walked to the table and slid into a seat without waiting for any further invitation.

"Granger," Kotler said. "Good to see you outside of a mountain for once."

Granger smiled and held up a glass of smoky amber liquid. A waitress arrived with Kotler's cognac, and he raised his own glass as if in a toast. "Roland tells me that authorities aren't too thrilled with you and your people," Kotler said, sipping his drink.

"We tend to leave that sort of impression," Granger said. "Occupational hazard."

"Detective Kozak wanted all of you brought in for questioning. Roland wanted all of you arrested on a laundry list of charges. I just wanted a crack at that vault, to see what else we could learn in there. Looks like all of us were disappointed."

Kotler had been informed almost as soon as he'd arrived back in New York that the vault had mysteriously been emptied before anyone could look into it. The military had arrived to take charge of the New Gods who were in captivity, only to find that neither New Gods nor Jani were present. The only people who remained were members of the SWAT team, who for whatever reason couldn't recall where the Jani had disappeared to.

Denzel had referred to it as *loyalty amnesia*. "And misguided," he'd groused. Though Kotler suspected he wasn't actually all that banged up over it.

"I think Mesa PD was grateful for your help," Kotler said.

"As we were for theirs," Granger replied. "I apologize that we had to evacuate the vault. But it's in a much safer place."

"Would that place be in Cheyenne Mountain?" Kotler asked.

Granger shrugged. "Who can ever really say for sure? Things have a habit of disappearing from history, at times."

Kotler accepted this. He knew that the Jani considered it their mission to safeguard some of history's most dangerous artifacts. He had wondered what they would do, with a trove the size of the one from Mesa in the hands of local law enforcement or, worse, a US Federal agency or military vault. Now he knew—there was never any chance that Granger and his people would allow that to happen.

"You might be interested to know that we've donated the copy of the Popol Vuh to a local museum, in the name of Ricky Miller."

Kotler raised his eyebrows, then nodded. "Thank you for that. I'm a little surprised, considering all the effort you went through to keep it out of the hands of Scope and his men."

Granger shrugged again. "It was never about the Popol Vuh. That was just the document that opened the door for the New Gods. It was something they could verify. Finding it meant finding the rest of what was in the vault. The more dangerous items have been made secure."

Kotler accepted that. "So what now? What brings you to Manhattan? Is there any New God activity here that we might need to know about?"

Granger shook his head. "No, nothing like that. I'm actually here for you. I'm here to invite you to join us."

Kotler had been on the verge of sipping his drink, and it hovered near his lips as he looked over the glass, gauging Granger's expression. He went ahead and took the sip. He let the cognac warm its way down his throat as he placed the glass on the table. It gave him time to collect himself, to consider and let all the implications set in.

"You ... want me to become a Knight of Jani?"

Granger nodded. "You've more than proven you are up to the role. You've trained, though we could likely help you improve a bit. Your knowledge of history and ancient cultures is profound. And you've proven more than once to be a match for the New Gods, as well as more than capable of solving the riddles of lost cultures. We encounter that sort of thing more often than you might think." He smiled, a note of irony in his voice. "In many ways, you're already one of us. I wanted to extend a formal invitation to make it official."

Kotler considered what he was hearing. It was an exciting proposition, he had to admit. And not something to be taken lightly, he knew. The Jani had resources around the globe. They had their fingers on the pulse of history. It was ... intriguing.

Kotler shook his head. "Granger, your organization—it operates in secret, and sometimes does things I find unconscionable. I don't know that I could reconcile that. Besides, I'm a publicly known figure. I'm not sure I could move unseen, as you and your people do. And I'm not comfortable with killing."

"You have killed before," Granger said.

Kotler nodded grimly. "I have. All the more reason not to make a habit of it."

Granger leaned forward. "We're aware of your fame, and your ... reservations. We feel you would be a remarkable asset. If you join us, I can bring you deeper into the organization. I can show you things you will hardly believe can be real. You would gain access to treasures and secrets that history has forgotten even existed."

"And what would all that access cost me?" Kotler asked.

Granger nodded. "There is always a cost. You would serve at the whim of the Jani. You would be sworn to secrecy, and to break your oath would mean death for you and, perhaps, others. You would walk away from relationships, from friendships and lovers and family. You would leave behind your life, as it is now, and embrace a whole new life, filled with the impossible."

"Leave everything and embrace a life of secrecy and shadow," Kotler said, shaking his head. "That makes me think you don't really know me at all."

"I know this would mean sacrifice for you," Granger said. "I also know it would mean finding something that is a deeper question within you."

"And what's that?" Kotler asked.

"Meaning," Granger replied. "Join us, and you will come closer to the meaning you've searched for since you were a boy. You will find answers that move you closer to solving the greatest riddles of all time. As one of us, you will be that much closer to what you really want most out of life."

Kotler studied him, thinking. He tossed back the remainder of his drink and put it down on the table. He reached into his coat to take cash from his wallet, and Granger waved him off. "It's on me. And please, think about the offer before you say no. Consider it. We have time. I won't wait forever, but I can give you time."

Kotler rose and squared with Granger. He looked down on the immense man and sighed. "You know, Scope made me an offer, too. He wanted me to join the New Gods. He promised power."

"Amateur," Granger grinned. "If he'd bothered to learn anything about you, he'd realize that you already have power."

"I think you've gotten some faulty research," Kotler said, shaking his head.

Granger laughed. "No, I know exactly what sort of power you have. You might not, but I do. I'm also aware of that offer from Scope, if you recall. I was listening, when he made it." He paused, studying Kotler's face, then said, "And I know about another offer, from your friend Gail McCarthy. She wanted you to join her as well, didn't she? To be part of her vast smuggling empire. To play Anthony to her Cleopatra? You turned her down as well."

Kotler didn't bother asking how Granger knew about Gail or her offer. The words of Scope still echoed in his ears.

Do you believe that the Jani have no presence in the FBI? Do you honestly believe that after all these centuries of infiltrating and influencing governments and organizations of power, that we would have neglected to place people into key roles in US law enforcement?

"So what makes you think I won't turn you down, too?" Kotler asked.

Granger grinned. "Because unlike those other offers, you didn't immediately say no. You hesitated. You told me that you'd think about it."

Kotler blinked. He stared at Granger for a beat, then nodded once before turning and walking away, through the bar and out into the Manhattan night.

He knew Granger would be in touch.

He knew the offer would stand for some time. He couldn't say for how long, but it didn't matter.

Because Granger had been right.

Kotler had hesitated.

Standing on the sidewalk in front of Hemingway's, he thought of calling for his fifth car of the evening. Instead, he decided he could use the walk. He pulled his coat closed, put his hands in his pockets, and started toward his apartment. It was several blocks, and it would give him time to think.

His phone buzzed, and he checked it to find a message from Denzel.

Got another case I could use some help on. It'll keep until the morning. Can you swing by?

Kotler let out a quick laugh and typed, *I'll be there. You can count on me.*

A NOTE AT THE END

Like a lot of writers, I have a collection of "false starts." It's a large collection, actually, encompassing huge chunks of hard drive and Dropbox space. For years I referred to most of these false starts as my "first thirds." They were usually the first third of a novel, abandoned when I hit a muddy point in the story.

I don't abandon stories often these days—and I especially don't have a lot that are abandoned after only three chapters. I've learned the value of sticking with it, to see where I turn up once I've mucked my way through the muddy middle and reached the other side. Sometimes I find I've ended up with a story far different than what I thought it would be when I started.

This was one of those times.

In a sense, I have all those false starts and first thirds to thank for my current author career. Back in late 2015, when Nick Thacker dared me to write and publish my first thriller novel, I drew on those chunks of abandoned story to help me get a head start. I figured if I already had a large chunk of the book written, I'd be more inclined to finish it.

Turns out I was right.

And that book, *The Coelho Medallion,* ended up becoming a defining moment in my career. It put me on a path that, though I hadn't expected it, has brought me more success and joy than I ever thought possible at the time.

Fast forward to now, and *The Spanish Papers* is another example of how a rough start can lead to something unexpected—a book that, I believe, is a notch above my previous work.

That's me saying that, and ultimately it will be up to the readers to decide. But while writing this story, I felt as though I were tapping into a deeper part of myself, applying lessons I've learned from producing forty-some-odd books and eight Dan Kotler books in particular.

The thing is, this book didn't start off well, and almost wasn't written. In fact, it almost wasn't called *The Spanish Papers* at all.

Originally, this book started as a short story titled "The Genesis Papers." I wrote the opening for it while I was sitting in my hotel room in Pittsburgh, a bit depressed and disgruntled over a bad experience I was having at the Nebula Awards.

At that time, I was working on the manuscript that would eventually become *The Devil's Interval,* my third *Dan Kotler* book, and I wasn't really feeling it. The story was interesting. I was happy enough to be back at it with Kotler and Denzel, and I was excited about the idea of our heroes discovering a lost technology among the papers of Sir Isaac Newton. At its heart, that book fit perfectly with what I believed to be the pulse of my series.

But I wasn't feeling it.

For a start, my experience at the Nebula Awards was

absolutely dreadful. Pittsburgh was a city I'd been to before, and I even have some extended family there. It was good to have a chance to meet and chat with friendly faces before facing the multitude of strangers I'd encounter at the conference. But that moment passed a little too quickly for me, and soon I found myself among hundreds of sci-fi writers, all looking for the "secret sauce" to success as an author, and all pretty much ignoring anything I said that didn't fit with their existing mental model of what publishing was.

These were good people. I want to put that out there right away, because I love meeting authors and people who work in publishing, hearing about their dreams and goals, and talking to them about the work. Even though I don't currently write science fiction, it was still exciting to be able to talk about future technology and other ideas. I was still thrilled to be a part of something I'd grown up hearing about, that had been a part of the careers of some of my favorite authors. It was a bit like standing among legends— though none of those legends had actually shown up to the conference or the awards. I'm not sure the Nebulas and the Hugos still hold the sort of sway they once did. But that's a topic for another day and another forum.

Generally, when I attend an author conference, I find my tribe. I find people who, like me, not only dreamt of writing for a living but actually went out and *did it*. I have an instant rapport with other writers. We have built-in enthusiasm and camaraderie.

But not at this conference.

For the most part, authors attending the Nebulas are focused on traditional publishing. They've spent large swaths of their lives thinking that the only viable way to be an author is to pass through as many gatekeepers as possible.

Run the gauntlet, survive, and you've earned your place. You may stand bloodied, you may be bruised, your strength and energy may be spent, but you've pleased the publishing overlords. You've proven yourself worthy.

I don't think that way.

I used to, don't get me wrong. But then, in 2008, I did something that changed the course of my life. After having turned away from a traditional contract, I decided I'd try my luck with self-publishing. And even though I was a little embarrassed by it and self-conscious about it at the time, I eventually figured out that this was the path for me.

This was empowering for me. This was me owning my career, from the quiet moments spent daydreaming about a story to the glorious hours of putting that story on the page, and finally to the exquisite triumph that only seeing your name on the spine of a book can give you.

This was me, doing what I always dreamt of doing, without waiting for anyone's permission to do it.

And. It. Was. Glorious.

Ok, so that's a bit of the start of my journey, and I'll admit there have been ups and downs.

While I was sitting in that hotel room in Pittsburgh, keeping to my discipline of writing every day, I started adding to *The Devil's Interval*, putting more story on the page, and continuing to do what I'd done every day for years.

And I just stopped.

The night before, I had been in the Green Room—basically, a lounge set aside for speakers and other official guests of the conference, allowing us to have a place to refresh ourselves, to grab a bite to eat or something to drink, to sit and chat with each other in peace. I was there for a spot of lunch. And as I stood with a plastic plate in hand, piling on salad and deli meats, a man beside me asked, "So how many books have you published?"

It took me back a little. I hadn't been expecting it. But heck, since he asked ... "Oh, around forty. I have a couple on pre-order right now."

"Whoa!" He replied. "Forty books! How many awards have you won?"

"Six so far," I said, smiling. "My most recent was the Shelf Notable Indie award."

There was a pause.

"Indie? As in indie publishing?"

"Yeah," I smiled, nodding.

The man literally turned his back on me, walking away to start a conversation with someone else on the other side of the room.

I kept smiling. Though, you know ... *dying inside*.

I'm pretty sure I ate my salad in silence. I know I had a scotch. And then I went back to my room.

It had been a long enough day. I had met enough people. I was good. The rest of that day's conference shenanigans could play out without me. I made a pot of coffee and read William Carlsen's *Jungle of Stone* for the afternoon, playing music and making a dinner out of a bag of almonds and a bottle of water I'd gotten at the airport. The world could turn without me for the evening.

And the next morning, I felt utterly worthless.

I started working on *Devil's Interval* just like I'd been doing steady for the past couple of weeks. I had published *The Atlantis Riddle* the month before, and I was trying to keep a rhythm going. But it wasn't happening. I was feeling dejected. Unmotivated. Worthless.

Maybe I needed something new? Something I could finish a little faster, so I could put a check in the "win" column in just a couple of days instead of weeks. Maybe I should start writing a short story between full novels, the way I'd talked about. Maybe that would reignite my spark.

I closed the file for *Devil's Interval*—making a deal with myself that I'd get back to it eventually—and I opened a new file. On a whim I called it "The Genesis Papers," because it sounded like it might have the right flavor for a Dan Kotler story, and for the next half hour I wrote about Ricky Miller and his discovery of a strange set of documents that, he hoped, might get him a spot on *Ancient Aliens*. You might recognize it as the very scene that opens this book. That much, at least, I kept. I was still feeling a little dejected and miserable, but at least I was making progress.

And then I stalled.

Suddenly I just wasn't feeling it. I just couldn't get myself motivated. I wanted to. I like being someone who finishes what he starts, who sticks to his commitments. It's part of my definition of self. But I had let something seep into my soul, there at that salad bar in the Green Room of the Nebula Awards. I had allowed someone else to have a say in my sense of self-worth. I had stopped believing in myself, just a smidge, and it made me unworthy.

I finished out that conference, and went about my life, doing the sorts of things an author does when he has a couple of books out but no mojo to write more. I tinkered. I felt oppressive guilt. I got angry and resentful about it and then felt *more* guilt over being resentful but not doing the work.

Of course, I'm no dummy. I knew then as I know now—writers write, and authors have written. I never actually stopped writing, though I wasn't producing books at the rate I had intended. I had started the year with a resolution of writing a book a month. That seemed doable, considering my track record. And it *was* doable if I put in the time and the work.

But I wasn't putting in that time. I was writing, but it was scattered. I wrote a lot of blog posts and articles and emails for the next few months but very few words went into the book that was on my board.

Eventually, however, I snapped out of it, at least a little. It wasn't too long after Pittsburgh that I decided what I needed was a fresh start. So I put Dan Kotler and Roland Denzel aside, for the moment, and I wrote two more books. Completely different books. Thrillers, but not Dan Kotler thrillers.

And they were good.

In fact, I love them. I think they'll be great. I think my readers will adore them.

But I haven't published them.

Because as a result of writing those two books, I managed to overcome the block I had installed in myself. As I worked on those, I started missing Dan Kotler. As I finished those books, I started thinking of the story I'd left unfinished. And so, better late than never, I got back to it.

I still wasn't writing a book a month as planned—that ship had sailed—but I was writing every day again. And in just a couple of weeks, the book I'd put off for months was done, and I immediately started the next one.

The Girl in the Mayan Tomb came from that burst of creative impulse, inspired by the real-life events explored in Carlsen's *Jungle of Stone*, which I'd been reading in Pittsburgh. There's karma for you.

There was another gap between *Mayan Tomb* and the next book, *The Antarctic Forgery*. For whatever reason, those two books were painful for me, and I had to drag them out of my brain, kicking and screaming. I love both of them, but they were a rough labor.

So rough, in fact, that as I started *The Antarctic Forgery,* I was right back to feeling that sense of depression and worthlessness. Worse, I once again stalled at the first third of a book—a condition I hadn't found myself experiencing in years. And just like Pittsburgh, I found myself wondering if maybe it was time for Kotler and Denzel—and perhaps even me—to retire.

And then I went to another conference, in Las Vegas.

It was almost as if God wanted me to see this thing from both ends of the spectrum.

Where the Nebulas had thrown me into a fit of depression, and I had begun to question my worthiness as a novelist, the Vegas conference opened up all the windows of my soul, and let in a gust of cool, fresh air. Though that was mostly metaphorical.

Here, nearly choked out by the cloying aroma of cigarette smoke that lingered like a fog bank over everything, developing the equivalent of a sixty-pack-a-day habit just by breathing, and surrounded by the most desperate array of slot machines and casino patrons you could imagine, I found my wings again.

I became so inspired by the talks, by the people I was meeting, by the charged environment of authors loving their craft, that I could barely wait. Every morning, every meal, every spare moment I broke out my laptop or iPad or iPhone, and I *wrote.*

I finished *The Antarctic Forgery* while I was in Vegas. And I kept the momentum going. I started writing *The*

Stepping Maze immediately after. I then wrote a short story called *The Jani Sigil* (which you can read for free if you join my mailing list at https://kevintumlinson.com/joinme). I wrote *The Stepping Maze*, which I consider one of my best books. And I started the book you have in your hands—a sequel to *The Jani Sigil*, and in many ways a symbol of my personal redemption as an author.

But recall, before it was titled *The Spanish Papers*, it was called "The Genesis Papers."

And yeah, there's a story there.

As a way to help me track the basic threads woven into this ever-growing series, I keep an elaborate note that contains all of my characters, the artifacts, the research, everything I have for each of my books. Someday it'll become too wieldy and cumbersome and intimidating, and I'll wish I'd kept it in a different, more organized way. But for now, it's my go-to resource for keeping track of everything I need to know. A lot of plot twists have come from scanning that note and remember so-and-so or such-and-such or reviewing this history or that thingamabob.

But sitting at the bottom of that note, like a sore that wouldn't heal, continually being pushed down as I wrote other books and other stories, was the tiny fragment of a note about "The Genesis Papers." It was my mark of Cain, my scarlet letter—the evidence of my greatest sin. The story I had yet to finish.

I'd tried. Believe me. I'd come back to it a hundred times, thinking each time that I would manage to tell the story. It was going to be the short story I gave to new readers, but then I wrote *The Jani Sigil*. It was going to be a standalone novella, but then I switched and wrote several more full-length novels. It was going to be a special fundraising story, but then ... actually, I can't even remember what happened with that one. I should do that, sometime.

Eventually, I figured I'd expand it into a novel. I started doing that, too, dozens of times. But before I got much further than describing Ricky Miller's shed, I was already feeling the weight of the thing. All the old dread and memories returned. I walked away. Again.

Then I had an interesting experience.

When I wrote *The God Extinction*, I made the decision that it would be a sequel to *The Brass Hall*. That novella had been the actual first story to introduce Dan Kotler to the world. I published it as a prequel to *The Coelho Medallion*, mostly so readers could have two books to read rather than just one. It was part of a strategy, and it worked well enough to call it a success. People who wanted more, after reading the novel, would invariably go looking and find that novella. It was a good way to tide everyone over until I managed to write *The Atlantis Riddle*.

The thing was, people loved that story, but they always had the same complaint: "I really wish this was a full-length novel!"

For three years I thought about that. I wondered if I should rewrite it and make it a full novel. I wondered if I should write another short, as a companion, and let them be a complete volume together. Eventually, I landed on expanding it into a fuller novel. It would mean taking a hit, Maybe causing some confusion with readers, possibly losing reviews. It wasn't a perfect solution, but I needed to make a decision and start writing. I wasn't going to lose momentum again.

I tried dropping that story into the first third of a new book, figuring it could be the opening chapters and then I'd leap ahead in time and write the rest. And for a few weeks, I worked at the new bits of the story, continuing where I'd left off, writing in a scene I thought could be a bridge between the original story and the new one, which I had decided would take place twenty years later.

I worked it for a couple of weeks, and even though I felt like I was trying to "pour new wine into an old wineskin," as the Bible says, I figured my readers would forgive the clunkiness of the thing and just be happy that they got "the rest of the story."

That idea was terrible. I realize that now.

The problem was that a lot had changed for Dan Kotler, in the three years since I'd written that novella. The character had grown and evolved. But so had I. With six other novels already telling the world who Dan Kotler was, I was finding it painful to turn back the clock for a third of the new book, to tell a story that wouldn't pick up the momentum of the series until four- or five chapters in.

I was making compromises. To bridge the gap between old and new, I wrote a vignette that functioned just like the prologues I write into the other books. This kind of worked —but it had the effect of making me stumble as a reader. Basically, the book contained one complete story—beginning, middle, and end—then all action halted, a random character appeared to incite a new incident, and *then* the characters we've come to love made their appearance. Of course, Kotler himself didn't return to the story until nearly three chapters later.

It was a mess. I knew it was a mess. The story didn't flow and didn't gel. The novella read like a bunch of random chapters glommed on to the front of a completely different book. It just wasn't working.

Eventually, I made the right decision. I yanked the story from that work in progress and went on to write the rest of

The God Extinction as a full-length sequel to the original novella. I decided that it would stand alone but make reference to that story—so anyone who read *The Brass Hall* would be in for a treat, but anyone coming in on that as their first book would still be able to follow the story. Both books would be independent of each other but still connected.

That's worked out pretty well, gauging by reader response. Reviews of *The God Extinction* have often mentioned its connection to *The Brass Hall*, making a special point of saying you need not read one to love the other. I consider that a check in the win column. Clearly, it was possible to write a full-length sequel to a shorter work and have both stand independent and strong.

And so that got me thinking: What if I did the same sort of thing for my short story, *The Jani Sigil*?

True, that story is only currently available to people who sign up to my mailing list. But I thought that maybe I could write the sequel in such a way that one need never read the short story if they didn't want to. I could write a standalone novel, and people could decide to get on my list if they wanted to dig a little deeper.

That was a good idea, I figured. It had the advantage of being strategic as well as allowing me to explore further something I thought of as intriguing. I liked it. I would go with it.

But what if I also pulled a thorn from my paw at the same time?

I took a few deep breaths, and I opened up my big, cumbersome note, and then stared at that line: "The Genesis Papers."

I opened the file I had for it and read through what was there—Ricky Miller's shed. The dread came back to me in a wave. The feeling of failure. The sense of unworthiness.

I breathed through it. I stood, I stretched, I shook myself.

I went back to it and, for the first time since writing those original scenes, I read them with an uncritical, non-judgmental, open mind.

Not bad. A good start.

I could feel the dread, though. The nagging anguish. The "you're not good enough" that haunted me every time I looked at this thing.

"Screw it," I thought. And I started writing.

I was a couple of chapters in when I realized that my original premise for this book wasn't going to work. Or, it would work, but I didn't want to do it. I knew exactly what story I wanted to tell, and the thread of this from the start wasn't going in that direction.

In fact, I realized with a shock that *this* was why I kept feeling that sense of dread! This was why I had put the story aside, avoiding it like broccoli on a plate full of cookies. It wasn't because I was unworthy or not good enough!

It was because it wasn't the story I actually wanted to tell.

I'd written something that was technically good enough but wasn't connecting with me as a storyteller. It was a good idea, a good story thread, but it wasn't right for me at that time. It wasn't time to tell that particular story yet. I had pages and pages of story going in the wrong direction, and subconsciously I was resisting it, stalling.

But writers have a superpower ...

We can edit.

Now that I knew what it was about this thing that was twisting my guts, I dropped back in to take a look at Ricky

Miller's shed, and to reexamine his first look at those papers, to rethink their contents. I decided, as I read, that I could make just a couple of small changes and that would correct my course. I could change a word here, delete a sentence there, and add some dialogue in that spot—

"The Genesis Papers" were no more. All hail *The Spanish Papers*.

Suddenly I had a wide-open playing field. I added some history I'd learned about the Spanish *División Azul*. In fact, I found the Spanish thread to be one I could pull and pull and pull, and it would keep yielding fruit. Once I changed the direction of the thing, new ideas were coming at me from every direction, and I started seeing a pattern I never even noticed before.

And the book flowed.

This book, the one that had stalled me a hundred times over the past couple of years, was *flowing*. And it was *good*.

So good, in fact, that I wrote the book in about fifteen days, with editing adding maybe five days. Not the fastest I've ever produced a book, but far from taking months as I had with *The Antarctic Forgery*, when I was struggling to break out of a funk I'd allowed myself to fall into, in a Green Room at a conference almost two years earlier.

Yesterday, my time, I wrote the final chapter and the epilogue for *The Spanish Papers*. I wrote both in a flurry of energy and glee. I knew the end was close, and it fueled me. I wrote like an inspired wizard, the world erupting from my fingers and onto the page like a flow of incantations.

This morning I edited those words and added 800 more besides. I tweaked some scenes, finessed some dialogue, and elaborated on some details.

And it was done.

It's been almost two years since I wrote that opening

scene. This book sat and waited for me to get my head and heart right, to come back to it with something I could offer. It waited until I had something to say—something I knew my readers (you) would want to hear.

From a moment of depression, even self-loathing, I've managed to come back, and come back strong. And now, I have no desire to retire anyone, much less myself. I have a new passion for this work, new fuel to drive me. It started at that conference in Vegas, back in November. But it's kept going all these months because of where that drive finally comes from.

It comes from a stronger and more stable place within me.

I can't promise that Dan Kotler's story will go on forever. I love him, and Denzel, and Liz and Dani and Sarge, all of them. But all stories, even those we love, eventually end.

Just not today.

There will be more Kotler books. And, if I have my way, other books as well. I'm looking forward to it. I'll eventually hit my personal goal of 12 books for this series, after which I'll continue writing it but will also pen other books, other series. This year is about focusing, getting my head and heart right, and doing the best work I can do for you and readers like you.

I owe it to you.

And I'm grateful to you.

I hope you enjoyed this book. If so, feel free to email me at kevin@tumlinson.net. And if you would like to hear from me from time to time, including getting some really great essays I occasionally write about the odd bits of history I discover in my research, go sign up for my mailing list at https://kevintumlinson.com/joinme. You'll get a free short story to enjoy, as a thank-you. It's a good one, too.

God bless, and happy reading.
Kevin Tumlinson
April 24, 2019
Sugar Land, Texas

HERE'S HOW TO HELP ME REACH MORE READERS

If you loved this book, you can help me reach more readers with just a few easy acts of kindness.

(1) REVIEW THIS BOOK

Leaving a review for this book is a great way to help other readers find it. Just go to the site where you bought the book, search for the title, and leave a review. It really helps, and I really appreciate it.

(2) SUBSCRIBE TO MY EMAIL LIST

I regularly write a special email to the people on my list, just keeping everyone up to date on what I'm working on. When I announce new book releases, giveaways, or anything else, the people on my list hear about it first. Sometimes, there are special deals I'll *only* give to my list, so it's worth being a part of the crowd.

Join the conversation and get a free ebook, just for signing up! Visit https://www.kevintumlinson.com/joinme.

(3) TELL YOUR FRIENDS

Word of mouth is still the best marketing there is, so I would greatly appreciate it if you'd tell your friends and family about this book, and the others I've written.

You can find a comprehensive list of all of my books at http://kevintumlinson.com/books.

Thanks so much for your help. And thanks for reading.

ABOUT THE AUTHOR

Kevin Tumlinson is an award-winning and bestselling novelist, living in Texas and working in random coffee shops, cafés, and hotel lobbies worldwide. His debut thriller, *The Coelho Medallion*, was a 2016 Shelf Notable Indie award winner.

Kevin grew up in Wild Peach, Texas, where he was raised by his grandparents and given a healthy respect for story telling. He often found himself in trouble in school for writing stories instead of doing his actual assignments.

Kevin's love for history, archaeology, and science has been a tremendous source of material for his writing, feeding his fiction and giving him just the excuse he needs to read the next article, biography, or research paper.

Connect with Kevin:
kevintumlinson.com
kevin@tumlinson.net

ALSO BY KEVIN TUMLINSON

Dan Kotler

The Coelho Medallion

The Atlantis Riddle

The Devil's Interval

The Girl in the Mayan Tomb

The Antarctic Forgery

The Stepping Maze

The God Extinction

The Spanish Papers

Dan Kotler Short Fiction

The Brass Hall - A Dan Kotler Story

The Jani Sigil - FREE short story from BookHip.com/DBXDHP

Citadel

Citadel: First Colony

Citadel: Paths in Darkness

Citadel: Children of Light

Citadel: The Value of War

Colony Girl: A Citadel Universe Story

Sawyer Jackson

Sawyer Jackson and the Long Land

Sawyer Jackson and the Shadow Strait

Sawyer Jackson and the White Room

Think Tank

Karner Blue

Zero Tolerance

Nomad

The Lucid — Co-authored with Nick Thacker

Episode 1

Episode 2

Episode 3

Standalone

Evergreen

Shorts & Novellas

Getting Gone

Teresa's Monster

The Three Reasons to Avoid Being Punched in the Face

Tin Man

Two Blocks East

Edge

Zero

Collections

Citadel: Omnibus

Uncanny Divide — With Nick Thacker & Will Flora

Light Years — The Complete Science Fiction Library

YA & Middle Grade

Secret of the Diamond Sword — An Alex Kotler Mystery

Wordslinger (Non-Fiction)

30-Day Author: Develop a Daily Writing Habit and Write Your Book In 30 Days (Or Less)

Watch for more at kevintumlinson.com/books

KEEP THE ADVENTURE GOING!

READ THE NEXT DAN KOTLER ARCHAEOLOGICAL THRILLER NOW

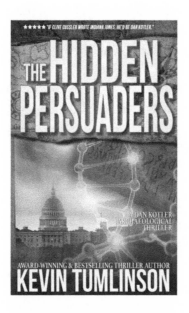

Read *The Hidden Persuaders*, the ninth volume in Kevin Tumlinson's hit archaeological thriller series!

Fourteen members of Congress have been abducted—in

broad daylight, right from the Senate floor. Kotler, Denzel, and Liz Ludlum race to uncover who is behind the abduction, and what ultimate threat they present!

The Hidden Persuaders is a pulse-pounding continuation of the adventures of Dr. Dan Kotler and Agent Roland Denzel.

See what readers and critics alike are saying about Kevin Tumlinson's Dan Kotler Archaeological Thrillers:

★★★★★ "Half way through I was waiting for Harrison Ford to leap out of the pages!"
—Deanne, Review for *The Coelho Medallion*

★★★★★ "Kevin has crashed onto the action-thriller scene as only an action-thriller author can: with provocative plot lines, unforgettable characters, and enough adrenaline to keep you awake all night."
—Nick Thacker, author of *Mark for Blood*

★★★★★ "Move over Daniel Silva, James Patterson, and Dan Brown."
—Chip Polk, Review for *The Atlantis Riddle*

★★★★★ "Move Over Indiana Jones, there is a New Dr. in Town!"
—Cycletrash, Review for *The Coelho Medallion*

★★★★★ "[Kevin Tumlinson] is what every writer should be—entertaining and thought-provoking."

— Shana Tehan, Press Secretary, U.S. House of Representatives

★★★★★ "I discovered Kevin Tumlinson from The Creative Penn podcast and immediately got his novel, Evergreen. I read it in like 3 seconds. It's the most fast-paced story I've encountered."
—R.D. Holland, Independent Reviewer

★★★★★ "Comparison to Clive Cussler is a natural, though Tumlinson's 'Dan ' is more like Dan Brown's Robert Langdon than Dirk Pitt."
—Amazon Review for *The Coelho Medallion*

FIND YOUR NEXT FAVORITE BOOK AT
KevinTumlinson.com/books

CPSIA information can be obtained
at www.ICGtesting.com
Printed in the USA
LVHW011422170520
655856LV00003B/642